"The entir... I'm buried here,"

Jackson muttered in utter disbelief, staring at his tombstone.

He could picture the funeral now. Weeping widow Emaline. Too blasted proud to admit he'd left town. He knew now he'd been wrong to give up and take off. But to do what she'd done. It set his blood boiling!

Well, he was back now to make amends. But it looked like Emaline had some explaining of her own to do. She'd be walking by the cemetery any minute now. He smiled in anticipation as he hid himself behind a huge, gnarly oak tree.

Jackson heard Emaline approach. The moment her moonlit shadow crossed his line of vision, he shot out to capture her from behind, his arms pinning her to his chest in a steely band. With a sharp cry she twisted around to get a look at her captor. The amazement sheeting her delicate, oval-shaped face was quite satisfying indeed.

"Honey," Jackson crooned in her ear. "I'm home."

Dear Reader,

Temptation is Harlequin's boldest, most sensuous romance series . . . a series for the 1990s! Fast-paced, humorous, adventurous, these stories are about men and women falling in love—and making the ultimate commitment.

January 1992 marked the debut of Rebels & Rogues, our yearlong salute to the Temptation hero. In these twelve exciting books—one a month—by popular authors, including Jayne Ann Krentz, JoAnn Ross, Leandra Logan and Candace Schuler, you'll meet men like Jackson—who demanded honesty from the woman he loved. Quinn—a hero to everyone except himself. And Brew—who'd fought his way off the streets.

Twelve rebels and rogues—men who are rough around the edges, but incredibly sexy. Men full of charm, yet ready to fight for the love of a very special woman. . . .

I hope you enjoy Rebels & Rogues, plus all the other terrific Temptation novels coming in 1992!

Warm regards,

Birgit Davis-Todd
Senior Editor

P.S. We love to hear from our readers!

The Last
Honest Man
LEANDRA LOGAN

Harlequin Books

TORONTO • NEW YORK • LONDON
AMSTERDAM • PARIS • SYDNEY • HAMBURG
STOCKHOLM • ATHENS • TOKYO • MILAN
MADRID • WARSAW • BUDAPEST • AUCKLAND

To Susan M. Johnson

A cherished friend,
a gifted author,
an honest woman . . .

Published May 1992

ISBN 0-373-25493-8

THE LAST HONEST MAN

1

"OH. IT'S YOU, LINDY."

The raven-haired girl in the colorful swingy dress did a double take in the bathroom doorway, nearly dropping the bundle of fluffy white bath towels in her arms. "Jackson Monroe?" she gasped, her dark eyes widening.

"Yep." The huge blond man seated in the steel claw-footed tub grinned around the long cigar clamped between his teeth. "Naturally, when I heard the bedroom door creak open out there . . ." he trailed off on a downbeat note.

"Well, you needn't act so darn disappointed," Lindy huffed, pursing her painted red lips.

"Sorry, little girl. Can't blame me for being anxious after all this time. And this is Emaline's room, not yours," he hastened to chide. "Naturally, I was expecting her right about now."

"Well, she sure isn't expecting you!"

"Why not?"

"Because it just can't be you, that's why," she said, blinking in sheer disbelief.

"Sure it's me, little girl!" he insisted, liberally sudsing his tanned, hairy chest with a bar of soap. "Jackson Monroe in the flesh. And in hot water, in more ways than one, I suppose."

Lindy watched him scrub and puff, the dreamlike lunacy of it all leaving her speechless. The tobacco smoke wafted above his wavy golden hair, lingering in the form of steel-blue thunderclouds against the pink seashell shower curtain backdrop. Her gaze sharpened as she studied the clouds, then his bearded, ruggedly handsome face.

It was an omen! A symbolic storm had indeed settled above Jackson Monroe. As a *poshrat*, a half-blooded Gypsy, Lindy knew about signs, hoodoo and talismans. Life was full of magical wonders, and she'd been raised to explore them without reservation. On stealthy bare feet she ventured inside the white-tiled room for a closer look.

"Hold it!" Jackson extended the gruff order with a drippy palm to halt her advance. "Freeze right there in your tracks, little sister. Or you'll soon be a whole lot wiser than your years." Knowing of Lindy's penchant for doing as she pleased, he grasped the pink plastic sheeting draped behind his shoulder to prepare for a hasty curtain call.

"Too late to pull anything over my eyes," Lindy retorted easily, hugging the towels to her chest. "I am sixteen as of this past July. I know plenty about love magic."

"You know only what your Aunt Verna knows," he grumbled, shifting his raised knees in the cramped quarters of the tub. "Yep, you know about love spells, charms, potions. If it's in her Gypsy bag of tricks, you know all about it."

"Gaujo fool," Lindy uttered, scowling to the tune of his good-natured laughter. Since when was her brother-in-law jovial about Romany lore? He did not believe in the Gypsy ways, had not wanted Emaline to believe, either. To Lindy, there were only two kinds of people in the world: Roms and gaujos—Gypsies and non-Gypsies. His sudden lightheartedness was incredible. What was she saying? His presence alone was downright cockamamy!

"What's on your mind?" Jackson broke in impatiently. "It's not like you to be so pondering."

"Why, the mere sight of you, Jackson Monroe, would make a lesser woman swoon into nothingness," she retorted in self-congratulation. "But rest assured that with my magic, I'm ready for anything." With a sly grin, she rubbed her cheek against the stack of towels.

"I doubt you're ready for any real results from those concoctions of yours," he said. "And, may I modestly add, you sure as shootin' are not ready for a look at what lies beneath these murky waters."

"I've seen things." A proud gleam lit her catlike eyes as she stood on tiptoe to peek over the edge of the tub. The water was too clouded with soap for any real revelations, however.

Jackson smirked knowingly as she settled back on her heels in defeat. "You've never seen this much of a good thing. Not here in Hollow Tree Junction, you haven't."

Lindy giggled suddenly, tossing her long mane of permed black hair behind her shoulders. "Still nothing modest about you, it seems, Jackson."

"I just believe in stating the truth, pure and simple." Jackson released a smoky chuckle, gingerly extracting his cigar with two wet fingers. "I'm an honest man, if nothing else. Words for my epitaph." He leaned forward to flick his loose ashes into the toilet bowl, but Lindy's shriek stopped him. "What's the matter?" he asked as she sagged against the vanity. "Did I say something wrong? I'm the same old brother Jackson you know and love."

"You just can't be," she cried insistently, righting herself on the floor again in a stubborn stance. "I wish it were so . . ."

Jackson cocked a brow, assessing her with concern. She certainly was riled. But wasn't she always in a tizzy about one thing or another? Living under this roof the first time around had taught him some valuable lessons on caution concerning the fair sex. He knew better than to let his guard down, even in the tub! "There's only one Jackson Monroe and you know it," he proclaimed flatly, his patience fading. "What sort of game are you playing, Gypsy girl?"

Lindy's full cheeks dimpled with knowledge. "I know that you're gone."

Jackson nodded sagely, returning the cigar to his mouth. "I was gone," he said between puffs. "But I've come back."

"You can't just come back! It's not done."

"I've done it. Jackson Monroe always does as he pleases." He took pause over her continued wariness. He'd assumed so much. Maybe way, way too much. But the third-floor quarters where he now sat appeared to be the same as the day he left. Some of his clothes still hung in the sachet-scented closet. Why, he'd have never drawn his own bath and stripped buck naked for a nice long soak, had he not believed this to be his place, too. "She's still here, isn't she?" he demanded.

"Sure, Emaline's still here. Hollow Tree Junction is our home."

"Good enough," he said, brightening with relief.

"She's never home on Friday nights anymore, though." Jackson grew still and intent. "Why not?"

"She's workin' at the Tip Top Café in town."

"Not Emaline!" he roared like a wounded lion, causing Lindy to inch back a step. "Why? You Holts go broke?"

Lindy fluttered her long black lashes in ignorance. "I don't know anything about the money. This is a big old house to keep up, I suppose."

"Your greenhouse still operating out back?"

"Uh-huh. Just like always. I don't know why Emaline took up with that evil-eyed Milton Dooley."

"So she's working for that pirate. I just can't believe it." Where was the money he'd been sending her every month?

"There aren't all sorts of jobs to pick from here in Hollow Tree Junction," she rambled on. "If you're not a farmer or a teacher or a nurse, there's not a lot of choice."

He knew it. How many times had he called this town of twelve hundred the end of the world? But what was his woman doing? Emaline of all people didn't need an outside job. She had her hands full with this rambling barn.

It had been a year ago last April when she'd commissioned Jackson, a handyman passing through Hollow Tree, to paint the family's three-story saltbox. He'd fallen off the ladder and broken his leg, cracked a few ribs. He was subsequently nursed back to health by Emaline. She'd given up her bed in this third-floor attic to him. Later on, the giving of her heart had followed. Lying in that bed, he'd planned how this bleak attic could be transformed into a master suite befitting a woman like Emaline—and a man like himself! He'd vowed to do something about it the moment he was back on his feet again—if being bewitched by Emaline could be considered landing on one's feet. He'd vowed to do something about her, too. The next time he landed in that bed, he wanted her with him! It had all worked out quite nicely. For a while . . .

Lindy watched his mouth tighten with anger. "I wanted to work the summer at the café, too, but Emaline wouldn't let me."

No, she wouldn't let that fat lizard tug at little Lindy's apron string. She'd sacrificed herself alone. But why? With his monthly contribution, the last thing he'd expected was to find Emaline in a financial bind. He hoped she would be in a physical bind, pining for him as much as he was for her. But the money angle had never once entered his mind.

"I really wanted to get out of the house," Lindy complained. "Everything that happens in this town is talked about at the Tip Top Café. I'm missing all the action, stuck back in our old greenhouse. Boring people buy our flowers."

"Hah! You're better off staying away from that place." Jackson zealously sloshed sudsy water over his broad shoulders, sprinkling the floor in the process.

"So you're really back, huh?" Lindy persisted, adoring yet doubtful.

"A man has a right to change his mind." His sonorous voice took on a soft reminiscent quality. "Has a right to realize he departed a bit too hastily."

"Lots of folks depart quick and never return."

"I'm not lots of folks." He compressed his lips in a hard line, balling his washcloth in a powerful handyman grip. Knowing that Emaline was right now down at the Tip Top Café with wily Milton Dooley made him dizzy with rage.

"Uh, Jackson?" she asked hesitantly, nibbling on a finger.

"What?" he asked, snapping out of his grim reverie.

"You come back naked?"

"What?"

"Well, did ya?" she coaxed, her dark eyes shining. "Tell me true now. Don't be bashful."

Naked? Bashful? Lindy Holt knew better in both cases. Jackson's gray gaze shifted in reply to the heap of clothing on the tiled floor. "I reckon few men are hearty enough to traipse around bare in the cool of a midwestern autumn evenin'. Your Nebraska breezes on the backside of September can be a bit chilly—on the backside!"

"You come right through the front door?" she drilled him in earnest.

Jackson cocked his head, eyeing her in confusion. "Well, no."

"No?" she prodded in open encouragement. "Tell me more, please."

"Came in through the back. The front door was locked." He paused with a frown. "When you start locking up?"

"Right after you left. Emaline didn't feel so safe anymore. Locked up her house and heart." She blew up her kinky black bangs. "So a lock stopped you, huh, Jackson?"

"I'm a carpenter by trade, not a locksmith," he retorted. "I could've kicked the door down, I 'spose.... Did it once up here. After Emaline slammed this very bathroom door in my face one night." A sentimental smile slanted his mouth. "Hope she doesn't do that tonight."

"No tellin' how she's going to take this," Lindy said. She tapped a finger on her honey-colored cheek, pausing in thought. "I wonder if she summoned you herself. Or if it was me?"

"Lindy, don't go on about lighting candles, or burying rose petals in the backyard," he cautioned. "I am not under some blasted spell!"

"I haven't put my heart into it in months . . ." she confessed, digging her bare toe into the tiles. "Maybe one of my incantations got caught up in the cosmos and just zapped you back here all of a sudden. Maybe you weren't meant to return, and I've unsettled the rhythm of the entire universe!"

"I got a hankerin' for my wife and changed course, little sister. No mystery to it."

Lindy grinned smugly, ignoring his theory. She and Emaline had both been well schooled over the years in the use of Gypsy magic by their aunt Verna. Jackson didn't just pop out of nowhere without a little help on this end!

Jackson shifted position in the tub, causing crests of water to peak near the top rim. It was a mighty small tub for a mighty big man. It was even smaller when he'd shared it with Emaline on sultry summer nights after their wedding. She'd had some exotic healing oil she'd rubbed on him during his convalescence after the accident. It had been very nice in the bath.... The thought of his eager young bride's slicked body riding his beneath the water made him ache with desire. "Why don't you toss me one of those fresh towels you've got, Lindy? Then mosey on out of here," he directed, waving a hand at the door behind her.

Lindy's face screwed up in disappointment. "You gonna put—"

"Yes, I am going to put my clothes back on," he interrupted impatiently, wondering if the kid had been staring at the quirky autumn moon too long. "Then I'm going into town to see Emaline at the Tip Top."

"You can't go there, Jackson!" she squealed, the towels dropping to the floor as her hands flew into the air.

"Has Emaline gotten herself attached to another man?" he demanded sharply.

"No, fool, no!"

"Are you sure she hasn't gotten tangled up with that wily Milton Dooley?"

"She can handle him," she insisted, dropping to her knees in the heap of white terry cloth.

"Then why the hell can't I go to her?" he thundered.

"How could you believe it would be so easy?" she chided in pitying exasperation. "Don't you understand, Jackson? You've been gone!"

"Has she forgotten me so soon?"

"You're not forgotten, Jackson. Emaline still calls your name in her sleep."

"Then she still loves me," he declared.

"Sure enough." She refolded the last of the towels, then sprang up to set them on the wicker shelf beside the vanity. "But you are still—"

"Gone, gone, gone!" he finished in a growl. "I'm here and gone at the same time."

"Jackson Monroe, are you as thick as a bedpost?" she demanded in a frustrated huff. "You are dead and gone! Have been since last February!"

The cigar in Jackson's gaping mouth dropped into the bathwater with a plunk and a hiss, missing the tender skin of his inner thigh by inches.

"The sight of you on Main Street would send God-fearin' folks into cardiac arrest. Especially poor Emaline!"

"I am not dead and gone!" He fished the soggy stub out of the tub with nerveless fingers, tossing it into the toilet bowl.

"You did so pass on, Jackson!" She pointed and stammered. "You—you kicked the bucket. Bit the big one."

"You really think I'm—"

"As a doornail." Lindy finished with a mournful look. "I'm sorry no one told you sooner."

"The blazes," he spat out bitterly.

"Funny you couldn't figure it out, Jackson," she murmured, her bright red lips puckered in sympathy.

He was sitting before her in the flesh, and the kid still believed he was dead! Jackson drew a breath, stroking his whiskered face. Of all the crazy... Did he really want to involve himself with the eccentric Holt family again? "Lindy, honey, my heart is beating," he reasoned quietly. "I am ticking along at a toasty 98.6."

Her expression of faith remained unshaken. "Where have you been, Jackson? Limbo? The blazes?"

"Texas, Oklahoma, Kansas," he reported, openly disturbed.

"You find your heaven, Jackson?" she asked in a hush.

"Only nice places to visit, Lindy."

"Look here," she scolded, her bangled wrist clinking as she shook a fist. "Emaline says you're dead, so you are!"

"Emaline said it?" His tone was lethal.

"Why, sure she did. Who would know better?"

Who, indeed? No wonder the fanciful Lindy was so certain of her facts. Lindy believed everything Emaline told her.

"Gave you a beautiful funeral last February," she continued on proudly. "Nice headstone, plenty of flowers."

He hadn't been gone a month and Emaline had buried him! The stubborn, mulish woman he'd regrettably left behind had killed him off, before he'd had time to kick Hollow Tree dust from his shoes. Probably eulogized him in the morning, then ran to the bank with his first monthly payment in the afternoon. But it was so unlike her. Unlike the woman he thought she was, anyhow. "Emaline wouldn't . . . She couldn't . . ."

"I can prove what I'm sayin'," Lindy said, a defiant lift to her chin.

"And you shall have your chance," he roared. "I'll have that towel I asked for now." She peeled one off the stack, teasingly tossing it just a little too high. He caught it with a long, sinewy reach, managing to remain tub bound. "On the count of three, I am leaving this tub," Jackson warned. "Get skedaddlin', little one."

"I'll cover my eyes," she promised solemnly. She raised a palm to her face, squinting at him through slatted fingers.

"One."

"Oh, what the heck difference does it make?" she whined in protest. "You're a ghost now."

"Two."

"Oh, all right." She spun sharply on her heel, causing her full bright skirt and long, frizzy black hair to swirl in her wake. "But you just wait till Emaline hears."

"Just wait," Jackson repeated as the door slammed behind her.

"JUST WAIT," Milton Dooley was also saying at that very moment a mile away at the Tip Top Café. "Hold on a minute, Emaline."

Emaline Holt Monroe weaved through the maze of wooden tables with slender grace, rounding the chipped orange counter with a pot of coffee in her hand. She washed the bitter liquid down the large stainless steel sink and rinsed the pot. "I'm tired and it's closing time, Milt."

"Oh, c'mon, let's have a cup of coffee and a cozy chat in the back booth," he invited, smoothing his button-popping peach shirt into the waistband of his black double knit pants.

"I just washed the last down the drain," she declared, not bothering to sound regretful. It had been a long, busy shift and she was as limp as her pink, food-speckled uniform.

"We'll go upstairs to my place, then," he persisted. "I'll draw the blinds, put on a Frank Sinatra record." He licked his lips and ran a palm over his shiny head. "You can take off your a . . . apron if you like."

"I believe I'll just be off to my own place," she declined in a light voice veiled in steel. Milt Dooley might have her over a financial barrel, but he would never ever have her lying over his barrel of a chest! Jackson Monroe had spoiled her for all men for all time. His lean, hard body and his hot, intense lovemaking had been her only taste of male attention, and it had left her dizzy with desire each and every time. This aging cynic left her only a little upset in the stomach. Emaline smoothed the blond hair secured in a knot at the nape of her neck, thinking how much she'd like to loosen it for the walk home. But one look at Milton's spreading leer froze her hand in midair. The owner of the Tip Top made no bones about wanting her for some amorous overtime.

"Stay on a few minutes, Emaline," he coaxed, clasping his plump hands together.

"No thanks, Milt," she replied, taking her white sweater off the tippy coat tree in the back corner.

"Tell me how your aunt Verna's cross-pollination is coming along," he tried, sliding along behind her in his shiny black shoes. "You know I'm just fascinated by all that flower stuff."

There was only one sort of cross-pollination that interested Dooley. Emaline paused at the entrance, her dark eyes scanning the plain, grease-tinged room with its orange-and-yellow booths, its chairs covered with shiny cracked plastic and its scuffed checkerboard floor. She hated this place, this man. Oh, how she wanted to take her apron and wrap it around Dooley's thick neck. But what a foolish dream it was! Thanks to Jackson Monroe. "Good night, Milt." Without as much as another look, she stepped outside and started down Main Street.

"GO AHEAD, JACKSON," Lindy dared, thrusting a finger at the headstone at her feet. "Tell me you're not a ghost."

Jackson was standing beside Lindy in the cemetery, his hands shoved into the pockets of his worn jeans. "The entire town thinks I'm buried here," he muttered in utter disbelief.

"Your name's on the stone," she pointed out with simple logic.

"Damnation!" Jackson thundered, kicking up the leaves blanketing the overgrown grass with the toe of his boot. He could picture the funeral now. Weeping widow Emaline. Too blasted proud to admit he'd left town. He knew now he'd been wrong to give up and take off. But to do what she'd done. It set his blood to boiling!

"What are you going to do, Jackson?" Lindy asked in hushed urgency, wringing her hands.

Jackson whirled on her, his teeth flashing white in the moonlight. "What time does Emaline get off work?"

"Café's been closed for a bit," Lindy said, with a glance at her watch. "Emaline should be on her way home by now. Passing this way real soon."

'Oh, really…" Jackson rubbed his whiskered chin. "Stay right here, Lindy," he directed, pointing to his plot. "I'll be back."

"Are you crazy?" she hooted rudely. "Do you have any idea how many spirits are flying around in here this time of night? This is a cemetery, you moron!"

"I'll just be up at the gate," he scoffed, gently cuffing her chin.

"So will I, buster!" she said, huddling close. "I'm sticking with you!"

"What if I turn out to be some kind of spook?" he couldn't resist needling, as she buried her cheek into the soft leather of his jacket.

"I'll take my chances," she murmured with a shudder, casting a stark look around the grounds.

Jackson clucked at the obstinate, wide-eyed teenager clinging to him for dear life. "How can a man have the element of surprise on his side with a hundred-pound Gypsy clamped to his middle like a belt buckle?"

Lindy drew a hesitant breath. "You going to scare her, then?"

"How can I? She knows I'm not dead!"

"How do you know she knows?" she wondered dubiously.

"She knows. This is nothing more than a joyous reunion." Jackson's tight smile belied his light tone, but luckily Lindy was too wound up to notice the contradiction.

"Emaline likes fun surprises," Lindy agreed with childlike delight. "Still . . ."

"This is a game for the big folks, little sister," he claimed, giving her head a pat.

"I'm old enough to join in any game. I am a mysterious woman."

Jackson shook his head. "You, little one, are a strange girl. Who is noisy enough to wake the dead," he added with a nose tweak.

"Let me come," she begged, squeezing him tighter. "I promise I'll keep my mouth shut."

"Oh, all right!" Jackson loosened her grip at his waist and began to march back up toward the gates. Lindy trotted behind him, content with tugging at his belt loop.

Glancing back from the entrance, Jackson had to admit that the cemetery did look eerie. The black iron gate was taller than the rest of the spiked fencing, meeting at the center in a sinister-looking peak. The nearly ripe moon was streaming down over the trees and markers, casting shadows across the lawns. He'd been so angry on the way in that he'd missed the ambience. Realizing now that an entire town assumed he was rooming here, he reflected that the atmosphere seemed almost threatening.

The gate was still ajar, just as they'd left it. With Lindy still hooked to him, he slipped through the opening and crossed the sidewalk to the boulevard, concealing himself beside a huge gnarled oak tree. Main Street ran horizontally three blocks up ahead, crossing the avenue on which they stood in the form of a T. There were old-fashioned lamps on every corner leading to the well-lit business strip, illuminating the area quite efficiently. Jackson had deliberately chosen the tree with the best cover. If only he could keep his sister-in-law quiet.

"Now what?" Lindy asked in a hushed stage whisper, which echoed over the vast harvested wheat fields across the street.

"We wait."

"What if we're already too late?" she wondered.

"It appears I'm about eight months too late," he said, thinking about how much fun it would've been to show up at his own funeral.

The click of heels from the next block startled them. Jackson stiffened, leaning forward to take a look. Lindy, to his annoyance, bent in unison just below him, her kinky black hair tickling his nose.

"Ah, it's just Miss Fricky walking her dog." She was obviously beginning to like this adult game a lot.

Jackson straightened up, inhaling deeply. The chilly fall air added an edge to his anticipation, causing him to shiver under his leather bomber jacket. His system was humming like a well tuned generator. His heart hammered and his muscles tensed as he readied to pounce. He opened and closed his fists, pumping blood through every vessel. He couldn't wait to get his hands on Emaline.

"Hey, it's her! It's her!" Lindy whispered, yanking at the sleeve of his jacket. "See, passing by Miss Fricky."

Jackson steered Lindy behind him and tipped forward on the balls of his feet for a cautious look. It was Emaline, dressed in a pink uniform with a white apron. She was crossing the street a block away, just beginning her journey along the length of the cemetery fence. Her maize-colored hair was pulled off her face, her head lowered against the breeze. A white sweater was set over her shoulders, closed at the neck by a single button. The empty sleeves hung free at her sides in a billowing, celestial flow. There was nothing supernatural about the look, in Jackson's estimation. He didn't believe in spirits and spells, in the hidden powers of the universe that governed three of the four Holt women like a tempestuous ruler.

Within seconds, Emaline was going to wish those flapping sleeves were wings, he thought wickedly.

Her low heels clicked along the concrete as she approached. Jackson had pulled back completely, using only his ears to track her progress. The moment her moonlit shadow crossed in his line of vision, he shot out to capture her from behind, his arms pinning her back to his chest in a steely band. With a sharp cry, she twisted her neck to get a look at her captor. The amazement sheeting her delicate face was quite satisfying, indeed.

"Honey," Jackson crooned in her ear. "I'm home."

2

"THAT'S RIGHT, sweet Emaline, it's your ever-lovin' husband. Come home to stay." Jackson stood behind her as solid as the mighty oak swaying overhead in the wind. He'd trapped her fast and hard against him, his words hot and triumphant in the sensitive hollow of her ear. She squirmed for freedom, her shoulders bobbing off his chest, her tight little bottom grinding into his crotch. The only thing she did manage to do was arouse him nearly to the snapping point.

Finding he could easily hold her with one hand, Jackson began to explore with the other. He loosened the knot in her hair, burying his face in the scented tangle for a long moment. His fingers roamed on, gliding a callused trail along her collarbone. She trembled against him as he popped open the top button of her sweater, causing the garment to slide off her shoulders to the leafy ground with a rustle. He palmed her breast through her thin layers of clothing, reacquainting himself with her softness.

Cries of dismay bubbled from Emaline in high, short squeaks, reminding Jackson of a small animal trapped in a snare. But she wasn't fighting him. As she writhed against his chest, he sensed a struggle raging within her.

She was battling her own desires.

Without a word, he continued his sensual journey, flattening his hand against her rapid heart, as if carefully counting the beats, then over the slippery fabric of her uniform, down the length of her rib cage. With a hand on her abdomen, he pressed her deeply into him. Jackson felt a surge of satisfaction as her lusty, covetous groan harmonized with his.

"Emaline Monroe, more proud than pretty," he crooned in her ear before spinning her around to face him.

Her shimmering dark eyes widened as she confronted his glare. "It was the other way around, as I recall," she said on an indignant gasp.

"That was before you buried me six feet under, my love," he growled, with a dangerous curl to his mouth. "So as beautiful as you are . . ."

"Is it him, Emmy?" Lindy broke in excitedly, circling the pair.

Emaline opened her mouth to speak, releasing only soundless, breathy puffs, which swiftly dissipated in the chilly autumn air. She stared at him disbelievingly, feeling the pulse at her throat weaken and weaken, until she swayed dizzily. Jackson held her more snugly, sensing her fears with a predator's cunning. A gleam of moonstruck madness silvered his eyes as he gently touched her face. Her nostrils flared as he slowly stroked the hollow of her wind-ruddy cheek.

Jackson still ignited her! Panic began to swallow Emaline as she tried to evade his touch, veering her gaze off into the black, infinite skies overhead. It wasn't right. Eight months of deprivation hadn't quelled her hunger for him. Her own system was at that moment totally betraying her, humming to life like a refurbished generator, aching for his touch.

She should indeed have killed him before she'd buried him! She pinched her lips together as his thumb traveled over her chin, tracing circles around her mouth. With a determined noise, he began to knead the tender flesh of her lips, rubbing them to swelling irritation. The moment her lips parted in a low moan, he pushed for entry, gliding the roughened ball of his thumb over her front teeth, exploring the moist, sensitive skin of her mouth with purposeful intimacy of time gone by. Through a veil of yearning, her eyes burned with denial. He wouldn't possess her completely. Not as he had before. Pressing the heels of the hands against his chest for leverage, she broke out of the circle of his arm. She reeled and landed on her bottom on the leaf-littered ground.

Jackson's dry snort of laughter crackled with the brittle rustle of the trees.

With an incensed cry, Emaline rolled to the side, quickly grabbing for her sweater. She flung it back over her shoulders there on the ground, swiftly jamming her arms into the sleeves. She looked up at him in defiance, buttoning like mad as if the light knit jacket was an impenetrable cloak.

His mouth curled sardonically as she fumed at his feet. "Come along, wife." One long-legged step closed the space between them. One fist on her uniform collar brought Emaline back to her feet. With a firm grip on her upper arm, he yanked her across the sidewalk to the cemetery entrance. Awestruck Lindy followed on their heels.

"I don't want to go in there!" Clutching at the bars of the squeaky gate, Emaline attempted to halt the procession.

"It's not your first time," he chastised, peeling her fingers from the bars. "For this or anything else!" He nearly swept her off her feet as he marched along, stopping only when he reached his own gravesite. "When you end a relationship, you really do it in style, don't you?" he asked in a strangled voice.

"You just don't understand, Jackson." She attempted to counteract his ferocity with teary softness.

He hated it when she wore that look. Vulnerable. Contrite. Gentle as a lamb with a hint of Gypsy fire flickering in her eyes. Those internal flames licked her eternally, constantly threatening to consume them both at any given moment. She was a hot, passionate wife, with a giving heart. With a reluctant hand, he smoothed the white collar he'd just crumpled. She was everything he remembered and more. More bewitching, more beguiling. Downright irresistible to the seasoned rambler he'd become over his twenty-seven years of life.

He'd dreamed of this reunion for months and months. The anger and resentment that had simmered over their marital disputes had dwindled with the passage of time, leaving him with only loving, lustful memories. How he had ever walked away in the first place was a puzzle. But it followed his own wandering pattern. His departure had been a predictable response to Nebraska's cold winter nights. Cabin fever pure and simple. Commitment and below-zero windchill had proven a sour combination. His footloose habits of a lifetime had sent him a-runnin'. But he'd learned soon enough he'd made a mistake. In the end he'd had to leave Emaline to discover that he truly belonged with Emaline. It was a lesson he'd hoped would be forgiven and forgotten.

Emaline was quite adept at the forgetting part, he thought, casting a nasty look at his tombstone. Forgiveness would probably take some work—on both sides. He couldn't wait to take her to bed. They communicated very well between the sheets. It was a place where he felt very much in tune with his unpredictable woman.

Oh, what a difference a little sex could make right

now. . . . Without another word he drew her against him again. He'd soon figure it all out, tear away her cloak of mystery.

Huddled against him, Emaline could feel Jackson shudder with tension. His huge carpenter's hand had risen to the column of her throat and was now caressing her skin with unsteady fingertips.

"Well, Jackson," she whispered, "you going to kiss me or kill me?"

"Maybe both." With a deep moan, he slid his fingers into her thick hair, guiding her head up for a crushing kiss.

Jackson Monroe proved to be a man consumed with an unquenchable thirst, which Emaline soon matched. His mouth took hers with flaming force. Cold air rushed through Emaline's nose and into her lungs, invigorating her. Her knees buckled as he drank her dry. When he did finally raise his face to draw a heavy breath of night air, she collapsed against his chest.

"Jackson, have you . . ."

"I've been true, if that's what you're wonderin'. Have you done anything more than bury me, woman?"

"No!"

"So, Emmy," Lindy broke in with youthful innocence, "can you tell yet? Is it really him?"

"Tell little sister, Emaline," Jackson ordered sharply.

"Jackson's back," Emaline conceded with a ragged nod.

"To stay," he added vehemently.

"Maybe I summoned you back," Lindy murmured to herself. "I tried the red jasper. But I sure didn't have any hot southern wind on my side . . ." she relented with doubt. "What do you think, Emmy?"

"I came back here of my own free will," Jackson bit out impatiently. Moving his mouth to Emaline's ear he added, in a low utter, "Here to claim what's rightfully mine."

Panic gripped Emaline. It had been so intense between them. Loving Jackson had taken every ounce of strength she had. Physically and mentally. She'd given herself completely to him. When he walked away, he had emptied her.

"You understand me, Emaline?" he demanded.

"Why'd you come back here, Jackson?" Emaline asked in a faraway voice, rubbing her arms against the chilly breeze rustling the trees.

"Blame it on our lucky full moon," he invited with a skyward wave. "The quirky harvest moon, only days away."

"Well, shame on the moon!" Emaline stomped her foot.

"Shame on you, Emaline," he admonished. "What kind of a woman buries her husband while he's still kicking?"

"What are you so sore about, Jackson?" Lindy broke in with genuine surprise. "You've been as safe as can be here on the south side of the cemetery."

"I've never been here at all!"

"You said you were never comin' back," Emaline chidingly reminding him, poking his chest. "And don't you dare try to deny it, Jackson Monroe!"

"I've mellowed some since then," he confessed. "But to do what you've done! And to think silly old me was worried about a divorce." He slapped his forehead with the heel of his palm.

"I couldn't just divorce you," she cried defensively. "Everybody would've been jabbering about how I couldn't hang on to a man. But I had to do something, didn't I? You just picked up and left me alone. I gave you some time," she attempted to justify herself, "telling everybody you were in Norfolk working on a construction crew."

"So how did this happen?" He pointed at his tombstone.

"Well, when I didn't hear . . . I had to end it all somehow!"

"So it was pride." He lamented with bitter triumph. "I thought so."

It had grown into so much more than that. Emaline's teeth sank into her tender lower lip, her mind racing with possibilities. Handling Jackson was going to take some cunning.

"You flat out lied to everybody!" He paced around, swinging his arms.

"I had my fingers crossed."

He froze, regarding her with open mouthed astonishment. "During the whole blasted funeral?"

"And a mighty fine funeral it was," Lindy broke in to report. "Darn near the whole town showed up. Even Milton Dooley."

"Dooley was here for my send-off?" he seethed. "You know how much I hate him, Emaline."

Emaline shrugged helplessly. "I couldn't pass out tickets. I couldn't stop anybody from coming. You were a curiosity from the start, with your loner ways and your fine handsome face. The cemetery was jammed!"

"You should've passed out tickets, Emmy," Lindy enthused, "like the circus!"

"It was like a circus? Have you people no respect?" Jackson paused in self-examination, stroking his beard. "This is preposterous! We're bickering about my funeral and I'm not dead! I hate lies, Emaline, I simply hate them."

"Look, Jackson, a twist of the truth is not always a lie," Emaline reasoned calmly, the drug of his lovemaking dulling some to give her sharp mind back its edge. "If something is nobody's business in the first place—"

"All my business is nobody's business."

"Unfortunately small towns don't follow the wanderer's code," she shot back sassily with a hand on her hip.

"Inventing tales is never the answer."

"You aren't even trying to understand," she wailed with a stomp.

"What poor slob could?"

"I—I just didn't know what to do," she confessed fretfully. "I hardly knew you. Then you left and I knew you even less."

"You knew me. I knew you." His voice was intimate, positive and determined.

"No, Jackson." She shook her head forcefully, staring at the ground.

He cupped her chin in his large hand, tilting her face to his. His eyes shimmered with raw need, the power of a man with a mission. "Well, regardless, you and I are going to be getting to know each other a whole lot better."

Emaline's breath lodged deep within her throat. He wanted to take her to bed. Jackson Monroe's cure-all. But they simply could not make love tonight. Maybe not ever again.

"Let's go home now," Lindy coaxed with a shiver. "This place gives me the creeps."

Jackson nodded, taking both sisters by the arm. "Yes, girls, let's go home."

"Don't expect to come waltzin' back into Hollow Tree Junction and my bed just like that," Emaline stalled forlornly, moving the back of her hand over her swollen mouth.

"I didn't come home for the Tip Top meat loaf, or for any of your auntie Verna's herb tea," he cautioned, openly confirming her suspicions. "You are my lawful wife."

"I don't need you," she claimed shakily. "Not like before."

"We'll just see about that, won't we?" he replied with smooth finality, tugging her along. "This honest man is bound and determined to make an honest woman out of you once more!"

"Mmm... Jackson. Feels...so good. You remembered...everything."

"Stroke the kitten and make her purr."

"Yes...yes!"

"The feel of your skin, Emaline. So supple beneath your silky stocking. Tell me it's still a stocking."

"A stocking..."

"So smooth. So easily undone."

"Just perfect, Jackson. Uh, except perhaps..."

"What is it, sweet?"

"Don't get sharp with me, Jackson. Your biggest failing has always been your suspicious nature."

"Forgive my wariness. Guess I've been living by my wits too long to be completely trusting."

"Ease your thumb up, Jackson. Oooh, just a tad more, please. Yes, my love. Oh, yes. Almost."

"Never just right for you, Emaline."

"Don't say that, sweet baby. Please."

"Damnation, how can I believe anything else!" With a strangled noise, Jackson shot up from the bottle-green brocade sofa, shoving Emaline's feet from his lap, the feet he'd been so gently massaging for half an hour. For the first twenty-six minutes, not a word had been spoken between them. It had been heaven. He'd thought he was really home again. But it seemed he wasn't alive in Emaline yet. He was still absent from her heart.

A sense of loss filled Emaline as she realized that she'd spoken out of turn. She was still dressed in her pink uniform from her shift at the Tip Top and smelled vaguely of café food. She didn't feel like a sensuous feline at all, merely a weary waitress. She stretched and groaned in discontent, pinning him with a greedy smile. "Jackson?"

"Don't give me that pout again, Emaline," he chided with a jaundiced eye. But it wasn't her pout that was capturing his attention this time around as she shifted position on the shiny patterned cushions. His eyes were now riveted to the slippery hem of her uniform as it inched farther and farther up her thigh as her long limbs unfolded.

"But you're not playing fair," she complained with a sigh, filling his vacated spot with miles of leg. "You give me a little, then you yank it away." Her voice dropped to a husky note when she added. "My feet have missed your tender touch."

"And what about the rest of you?" he demanded, hoarse with hunger.

"Start from the bottom now and work your way up," she suggested, rotating a foot in the air.

"Do it right here? In the parlor?" His tone held boyish enthusiasm, but his mouth slanted in roguish anticipation so blatant that Emaline's feminine core suddenly flared with heat, as if he'd struck a match to her pilot light.

"Of course not!" Emaline protested in a rush, causing him to freeze in midstep. "I didn't mean that far up."

"Oh, I see!" Jackson flailed his hands in the air, storming around the room. "Work my way up your arch, maybe to your toes, if I'm a lucky man?" He whirled to confront her willing his eyes away from the bow of her inner thighs. He could see the dark edging of her stockings and the curve of her hip. Her delicate skin was allergic to the coarse polyester of panty hose, so she wore smooth silk on those luscious limbs. A man could get lost in that shimmery web, he knew. He'd been there and back before, many, many times. The first trip had been the farthest, starting with a detour up the altar of the town church. Emaline had made the request and he'd been too doped up on passion to say no. But he didn't regret it. He only wanted to make things right.

"Let's just take things slow this time, sweet baby," Emaline prompted softly, tugging her dress back down to her knees. "Seeing you here has been quite a shock."

Sweet baby. He melted every single time she called him that. With steely determination he managed to disguise the tender tug at his heart behind a rueful retort. "It's not every day a man sees his own grave."

"Please believe I had good reasons for buryin' ya," Emaline beseeched. "Trust me."

"I thought . . . I hoped," Jackson stumbled over the emotional land mine within him. He knew he'd have to get it right to reclaim her. He just hadn't expected to find himself canceled like a stamp. "You have to be the proudest wife on the face of the earth to do what you did!" In the wake of the protestation that followed, he stomped across the faded blue-and-burgundy needlepoint rug to the carved rosewood cupboard in the front corner of the room. He opened the stained-glass doors with easy familiarity, encouraged to find that they still squeaked. No other handyman had oiled these hinges. And, thankfully, his bottle of Jack Daniel's was right where he'd left it last winter, second shelf behind Aunt Verna's crystal ball. The stout green glasses were still on the shelf above.

Jackson scanned the parlor as he cracked open the bottle. Not much had changed around the house. Cozy comfort of yesteryear with dark woodwork, hardwood floors beneath the fringed rugs, twelve-foot ceilings and tall Victorian windows. The two-tone brown paint job he'd given the outside had held up well too—at least by moonlight. Ah, that paint job. The place where it had all begun . . .

"Let's have a nice homecoming," Emaline proposed, sitting up on the sofa.

Jackson poured himself a finger of whiskey and drank it, watching her over the shade of the Tiffany lamp across the room. Her loose, flowing hair gleamed in the low light, wild and windblown from the walk home. Her face was flushed to an attractive pink, her lipstick smudged. She looked disheveled, appealing and secretive in a way that only she could.

There was no question why Jackson had married her in the first place. Emaline Holt Monroe was the most generous, sensuous creature he'd ever encountered in his nationwide travels. A unique blend of Gypsy caprice and German stability rolled into one beautifully wrapped package. Twenty-four years ago her father's Gypsy family had come through town with a traveling carnival. Twenty-three years ago Emaline's fair, sensible German mother, Margaret, had given birth to the baby Emaline.

Not only had her dark, dashing father settled down in the small town of Hollow Tree Junction, but his sister Verna had, as well.

Perhaps fanciful Emaline had seen history repeating itself in the form of wandering carpenter Jackson Monroe, had fallen hard and fast for a nomad like her own absentee father. He hadn't asked at the time. He wanted her, so he took her. Perhaps he was being too harsh with her now for erasing him from her life. Perhaps her ultimate refusal to hop on his motorcycle and chase his dream had been too much to ask of a small-town girl. There were obviously so many secrets she was holding back now, as she had then.

"What are you thinking, Jackson?" she broke in softly.

"Of only you, Emaline," he admitted with a road-weary sigh.

"Bring the bottle, Jackson," she invited, stacking magazines on the end table. "And the glasses."

One hour and a half and one half-empty bottle later, Emaline was rubbing Jackson's bare feet.

"So you see, Jackson, it's just that simple," Emaline explained to the dozing man stretched out on the sofa. "I hoped and hoped you'd reconsider your hasty retreat and come back home. When you didn't, I realized I had to do something. You know how nosy people are. It was the same old question in town every day. Where is your husband, Emaline?"

"Uh-hmm..." Jackson flexed his thighs, shifting his narrow hips. When Emaline stopped rubbing the feet plopped in her lap, he wiggled his toes for attention.

"I couldn't bear to face everybody here, people I've known all my life, if they thought I couldn't hold on to a man." She blinked and sniffed and continued the massage. "It just wasn't fair, Jackson! You drifted into my life,

my cozy space here in Hollow Tree, then left me lookin'
like the fool."

"I wanted you to come with me, Emaline," he grog-
gily argued, struggling to keep his eyes open. Between the
liquor and his lack of sleep, he was sinking fast.

"Oh, sure, give up my life here to live on the wind! You
just don't understand about family because you don't
have any. There are obligations to consider. One in particular that you unintentionally dropped right into my
lap. I imagine you've left messes behind in the past. But
you forgot that you left me behind to face it this time!"
Emaline's tone and thinking were both as clear as a bell.
Her conservative drinking habits, coupled with the fact
that her adrenaline was flowing furiously through her
veins, left her as sharp as a tack. "To tell you the honest
truth, I'm having a bit of a problem respecting your claim
on honesty!"

"Let's go up to bed now, honey," he suggested thickly,
resting a hand on her knee. "I'll make it all up to you.
Honest I will."

"You have a one-track mind, Jackson Monroe," she
scolded, flicking away his creeping hand. "And I believe
you hardly heard a word I said." He struggled to sit up,
but flopped his head back on the pillows in total exhaustion. Within seconds he was asleep, drawing air
through his nose with a low rhythmic snore. She eased
his feet from her lap, gently rising from the sofa. "With
your libido, how will you ever be able to handle the har-
vest-moon curse upon us, my darling?" With a last regretful look at his ruggedly handsome face, she tiptoed
out the parlor.

"Emmy!" Lindy called from the kitchen doorway at
the end of the narrow hallway.

Emaline gently closed the sliding pocket door behind her, then turned to her sister. "Shhh! Jackson's sleeping."

Lindy's round face grew somber. "Just how deep are we talkin'?"

"He'll be waking up in the morning, if that's what you mean," Emaline snapped. Instantly sorry she added, "I'm just a bit jittery tonight, I guess."

"These things don't happen every day," Lindy sympathized, pattering up the hallway. "How did you get him back? Did you kiss the amber stone, sleep with it under your pillow?"

"No, I did not," Emaline claimed with a firm shake of her head. "Any sign of Mother and Aunt Verna?"

"It's only a bit past nine. You know the Bingo Palace in Edgerton is open till eleven."

Emaline closed her eyes and rubbed her temples for a long moment before responding. "Yes, I know. But Mother didn't really want to go at all. When Aunt Verna drags her somewhere, it can turn into a late night."

"It's all right," Lindy soothed. "Colin was meeting them at the Palace. You know that will keep Mother in her seat."

"They've both certainly taken a shine to our British neighbor."

"Imagine, both Mother and Auntie in their fifties, having a rivalry over that cheap limey," Lindy scoffed. "Well, it'll work to your advantage tonight. Neither one of them is about to leave the other behind to ride home in Colin's car. You're safe for now."

"Safe?" Emaline rolled her eyes.

"So, tell me what you did," Lindy persisted. "Wear a linen bag of rosemary?"

Emaline gazed into her sister's wide, sparkling eyes and spoke firmly. "I did nothing."

"But Emmy, it had to be one of us."

Emaline gripped Lindy's shoulders, giving her a gentle shake. "I didn't bring Jackson back and neither did you. Not from beyond, not from Norfolk, not from anywhere."

"You're wrong," Lindy argued with implicit faith. "Found him myself, right smack-dab in your third-floor bedroom suite, sittin' high and mighty in your old tub, naked as the day he was born!"

"You did?" she demanded, momentarily sidetracked. The buzzard had used her tub! It could've been a far different reunion had she found him there. Which was what he'd intended, of course. He knew very well she'd always enjoyed Friday nights at home.

"Don't worry, Emmy," Lindy consoled, misreading her sister's scowl. "I didn't see a thing. Not that I didn't want to . . ." She shook her frizzy black head, the dimples in her cheeks deepening with her smile. "You know that Jackson claims he's got something more than any man here in Hollow Tree Junction. It was all his fault, telling me that, then shooing me away. All his fault."

"It's all his fault, all right." Emaline wandered into the spacious front entry hall, trying to piece together the proper words. She'd never lied to her little sister before Jackson. Hadn't done so since, unless it was on the subject of him.

"Well, what did bring Jackson back?" Lindy stood at the foot of the open staircase, one hand clutching the ornately carved newel post.

Emaline met her worshipping, expectant gaze with a wan smile. "I can't take the credit—or the blame—for Jackson's return. He's acting on his own."

"How you can be sure none of your spells worked?" Lindy persisted. "You're way too modest, Emaline. Your powers are strong enough. When you put a mind to it."

"I know because I never tried to bring him back, Lindy," Emaline confessed with emotion, turning away from her sister's shocked expression. She stared at her own reflection in the large mirror on the wall beside the closet door. Exotically shaped onyx eyes and sculpted cheekbones set in a model's oval face reflected back at her with a wizened womanly look, making her appear older than her years. She did feel quite wise at times, but worldly Jackson had a way of making her feel small and naïve. It was going to take a lot to stand up to his demands and rantings. But if she wanted him back, she had to try.

"But you used lots of spells on him before and after the marriage," Lindy recalled in confusion.

Emaline nodded. "Yes, I did. But I soon learned Jackson has a will of iron. I knew there wasn't a spell strong enough to hold him, in the end."

"But you must've been tempted to try, weren't you? I can't believe you gave up on the only man you loved just because he crossed over."

"You've got it all turned around, Lindy. First of all, I don't have the power to bring back a man body and soul from the other side. Even if Jackson had died, which he didn't," she reluctantly added, "I couldn't have pulled off such a feat."

"You're talking riddles," Lindy squawked in exasperation. "Of course he passed on. He just doesn't know he's a ghost."

"Jackson never really died. I merely pretended he did. Buried a coffin full of rocks six feet under for the whole town to see. Now, wouldn't I have been the fool to start trying to lure him back here just to make a mockery out of my widowhood? No, once I'd buried him, I was stuck with my decision. No matter how much I'd have liked to lure him back."

"Why not say he ran off? Just in case he decided to come back someday?"

"He said he was never coming back. And he meant it," she added adamantly. "Just like . . ."

"Just like our own father," Lindy finished with a sigh. "He sure disappeared for good."

"We just couldn't have stood the shame of losing a second man around here. Folks would've said we're cursed. Stopped buying our flowers in the greenhouse."

Lindy's face fell. "I can't believe you didn't tell me. I thought we shared all our secrets."

"No one ever shares all their secrets, little one," she whispered, stepping forward to pinch her chin. "This thing with Jackson. It's really gotten complicated, more than I can say right now."

"Does anyone know?" Lindy asked, her perky features drawn in hurt.

"Of course not," Emaline assured her. "It's my own secret."

"I wish you'd have trusted me, Emmy."

"I plan to trust you now. But you must do exactly as I say. . . ."

Fifteen minutes later, Lindy joined Emaline in the parlor, a shoe box brimming with the items her sister had requested.

"Help me with him," Emaline huffed as she wrestled with Jackson's mighty shoulders in an effort to remove his powder blue work shirt.

Lindy set the box on the coffee table and dropped to her knees beside the sofa. "Ooo, he's sweet enough to gobble up," she purred as she pulled the cotton fabric away from his solid chest.

"No question about it," Emaline huskily conceded, her fingers gliding through the nest of tawny hair on his taut stomach.

"Why didn't you steer him up to bed while he could still navigate some on his own?"

"Because, because," Emaline began, only to falter. She leaned over to drape his shirt across the arm of a chair.

"It's like candy, isn't it?" she eagerly pursued. "One taste and you're hooked."

Emaline agreed on a wistful murmur. Her sweet baby's lovemaking was addictive. Flowing tides of sweet, sweet sugar.

"I imagine Jackson's pretty good at it, isn't he?"

"I can't imagine more," Emaline confessed.

"Then why not, Emmy? So what if Mother and Aunt Verna think he's dead? They're miles away wooing Colin and screaming 'Bingo!' You could've had your fun for ages yet."

"I imagine you're old enough to know the answer," Emaline declared after some contemplation.

Lindy scrambled to her feet, alight with treasure-hunt anticipation.

"The moonstruck curse that destroyed our parents' marriage struck a second blow in the Holt family," Emaline blurted out painfully.

"No!" Lindy clapped a hand to her mouth in genuine surprise.

"We made love by the light of the harvest moon last September, just as Mother and Father did years ago. Jackson left soon after, just as Father did."

"Poor Emaline," she cooed, stroking Emaline's hair.

"Aunt Verna's been schooling us on that curse for so many years," Emaline whispered, brushing aside the tears on her cheeks. "I just never thought it could affect our generation as it has. If I make love to Jackson, I will surely lose him again.... Perhaps never to return!"

"You must talk to Aunt Verna about a cure," Lindy advised, giving her a squeeze.

"I can't. For many reasons, it is impossible."

"But why?"

"This is no time to ask questions, Lindy." Emaline closed the issue, turning her attention to the box on the table, crowned with a folded steaming towel. "Did you find everything?"

"Oh, sure."

Emaline sat on the edge of the sofa cushion and pressed the moist hot terry cloth over the lower half of his face.

"You ever shaved him before?" Lindy wondered, hovering over the proceedings with a doubtful frown.

"No."

"You've covered his mouth. Can he breathe?"

"He breathes quite nicely through his nose," Emaline retorted, thinking of the heart-stopping kiss he'd given her in the cemetery.

"What if he wakes up? With his temper..."

"He's in a drunken stupor. He'll be out for quite some time."

"Are you sure you're doing the right thing?"

Emaline shifted her hip against his arm, fingering a tuft of his coarse blond hair. "We're doing the only thing."

"Would it be so bad if folks found out he was back, Emaline?"

"Yes, Lindy," she clucked in regret. "In the case of some folks, it would."

3

JACKSON AWOKE the following morning with a splitting headache. Twisting his body on the cramped Victorian sofa, he soon found that the pain shot clear down his spine to his toenails. Not the sort of homecoming he'd planned on in the roomy four-poster bed where Emaline had no doubt spent the night. The thought of her traipsing up two flights of stairs to the third floor, leaving him behind in drunken exhaustion, drew forth another sort of ache altogether. Would she ever be able to forgive him for leaving?

Gritting his teeth, Jackson swung his legs over the edge of the cushions to an upright position, pushing aside the lavender-scented afghan covering him. Ever so gently, he lifted his chin off his chest and slowly looked around the parlor. The musty room was nearly as dark as it had been the night before. If not for the telltale sliver of sunlight slicing in between the burgundy velvet draperies, the scene would've been timeless. That was what Hollow Tree Junction was to Jackson. Timeless. Changeless. Everlasting. For a lifelong drifter thrilled by constant motion, it had been a prison as claustrophobic as a high security cell.

Emaline, too, remained the same. Still bewitching. Still beguiling. Still too beautiful for her own good—or more to the point, for his own good! He just couldn't stay away any longer. Couldn't bear to legally terminate a union that had proven to be the best thing that had happened to him. So why had he spent the night twisted up like a pretzel on this archaic historical monument when there was a perfectly cozy spot upstairs for the husband of Emaline?

It literally hurt to think, but Jackson forced himself to mentally retrace his steps during the past twelve hours. The old steel bathtub upstairs had been the last place he'd had a rational thought. Jackson rubbed his temples with a groan. Lindy had accused him of being a ghost or something. Or had she believed him reincarnated? Was there even a difference, in that sprite's mind? Then they'd gone to the cemetery to look at his grave. Oh, yes. Then Emaline took him home for whiskey.

Well, an honest man such as he, had to admit the Jack Daniel's was his idea. But it was clever Emaline who'd improvised, pulling a switcheroo on his seduction schtick. When she'd agreed to a drink, he figured he was halfway to bed. Two glasses of whiskey and Emaline would've been pliable, agreeable, cordial. Yes, that had been the plan as he set the bottle down before her. One glass of Mr. Daniel's. Then another. One plus one plus one plus . . . An easy equation for seduction.

Jackson stood with a mighty rumble of discontent, stretching every fiber of his sturdy, six-foot frame. He paused in midgrowl however, feeling disoriented beyond his usual hangover symptoms. Things were different. Peculiar. For starters, his shirt was off, neatly draped over a nearby chair. But how? Why? Absently rubbing his hairy chest he flipped back the scenes, back through his befuddled brain. Had Emaline succumbed right here in the parlor . . . No! He'd remember that, despite the whiskey. And what about that whiskey? He cast a sharp look at the half-empty bottle and stout green glasses still on the coffee table. He'd tipped a few, but he couldn't recall her even finishing glass number one. Hmm ... He gritted his teeth, drawing air into his cottony mouth. Something was driving him crazy, but it was just beyond his consciousness, working its way into the foreground.

That was when Jackson reached up to stroke his whiskered chin, only to find it as bare as a baby's backside!

Jackson's hands flew to his cheeks, roving the exposed skin with stinging slaps. The pain in his head exploded as his heart thudded out of control. He stumbled forward, his whiskey-weary brain reeling. He swayed light-headedly, grasping the back of a nearby rocker for support. His precious beard was gone, he was shaved to his very brows! He stumbled a few steps more, fingering his bare, sensitive face, despite the prickly pain it caused. Maybe if he rubbed long enough, he could summon back the dense stubble, like a genie from a lamp.

Good lord, he was going mad! Magic wasn't his style. That was one issue on which he and his superstitious wife parted company. Emaline believed in everything from herbal potions to the phases of the moon. Jackson's agitation escalated as he paced faster and faster. Think, think, think! he prodded himself through his stupor. No one just lost track of half a face of hair. Only a single night had passed. It didn't seem plausible. But it wasn't only the beard, was it? Jackson himself was supposed to be gone—in his entirety. Maybe he was evaporating, with his whiskers the first to go.

Naw, it was one of them. A Holt woman had sliced him bare. Emaline? Little sister Lindy? Mother Margaret? Aunt Verna?

Swearing, Jackson marched to the dark pocket doors, sliding them open with a whack. "Emaline!" he summoned, barreling into the front alcove.

"Jackson." Emaline's whispered greeting from the open staircase cut short his attack. Whether she was simply on her way down the stairs or waiting for him to barge out of the parlor was not clear. She was a translucent image with her face free of makeup, her exotically tilted eyes shining onyx, her long blond hair brushed to a sheen. A German Gypsy dressed in a floor-length peach negligee and robe. No wonder he was mixed up!

Jackson stormed the staircase. She waited calmly on the bottom step, exactly his height with the added lift beneath her slippered feet. Jackson found he liked standing eye to eye with Emaline. She was not going to miss the murderous gleam in his gray eyes, or the dangerous pitch to his heavy brows. "We gotta talk, wife."

"Of course," she murmured, attempting to step down past him.

"Now." Jackson grabbed the tops of the posts at her sides, barring her path.

Emaline inhaled sharply as she met Jackson's abrupt blockade at chest level, one high, rounded breast grazing his solid biceps. Her nipple immediately hardened beneath the fabric of her negligee, a satiny pebble against his skin. Jackson couldn't help but think of a peach ripening before his eyes as he gazed down into the open robe. Her chest was heaving as she drew back with a hushed cry. He saw the fleeting ache in her expression. Why was she holding back her favors?

Jackson froze in his tracks, shuddering with a pang of desire that momentarily blacked out all forms of reality, including his missing beard. His eyes were fixed on the two soft fleshy mounds straining the stringy straps of her gown. Lusty memories traveled to his groin. His fingers tightened around the knobbed posts, kneading the smooth dark-stained wood. He knew if he lost control now, he might as well be buried six blocks away beneath his headstone.

"I know what you're thinking, sweet baby," she began, hastily closing her robe, securely knotting the sash.

"You'd be flat on your back in a dead faint if you really did."

"That's no way for a husband to act," she peeped in dismay.

"You don't know the first thing about being a wife, either."

Emaline studied his fierce face, considering his severe words, wondering just what riled him the most. "You still mad about being buried?"

A growl began in the pit of his stomach and shot up through his throat.

"Shh!" She pressed a finger to his lips.

Jackson nibbed it naughtily and leaned into her, his tone conspiratorial. "I'm learning to live with the news of my death. It seems, though, that I misplaced my whiskers during the night. Have you perchance seen them?"

"Is it an important loss?" she quizzed with a twinge of doubt.

Jackson nodded firmly. "I am disturbed to bone-rattling proportions," he confided in a strained whisper.

"I believe you look rather handsome this way," she complimented graciously. "Very gentlemanly."

"I no doubt look the fop," he snorted in contempt.

"You are too hard on yourself."

"No, wife, you are too hard on me! That is, if you are responsible for this atrocity."

"All right, you want a confession? I did it."

"Is this some sort of revenge, Emaline?"

"I merely did what I had to do," she claimed, leaning back a little, only to find no escape. Jackson's face was so close to hers that she drew his breath when she inhaled.

"There are codes about such things."

"Codes?"

"A good wife never, ever shaves a man's beard without permission," he recited, as if quoting the Constitution from memory.

"Maybe I wasn't a wife long enough to get the hang of it." She tossed her head defiantly.

"No, no, you probably know lots more about playing the widow," he snapped snidely. He fought for control of his emotions, a battle he was swiftly losing. "You don't get it, do you? You've done the unthinkable! Does a hen pluck a rooster's feathers?"

"Let me smooth your ruffled feathers, sweet baby," she whispered, raising a finger to his cheek.

"No!" With a pained yelp he jerked his head back out of reach. Her nail had barely scraped his raw skin, but it was enough to send a shudder through his body. So now she knew. The blade had left him tender, vulnerable. "There's nothing left to ruffle," he told her coldly. "Nothing left to stroke."

Her hand moved to the newel post, covering his. "I must tell you why, Jackson," she said contritely. "Please listen."

"Why?" he repeated incredulously. "Because a bird flew across your shadow at the stroke of noon. Because you stepped on one too many cracks in the sidewalk last week." She opened her mouth to protest, but he continued on. "I don't give a tinker's damn what kind of hocus-pocus explanation you're going to lay on me now. I had that beard for nine of my twenty-seven years, Emaline. It was a part of me. It was history. The history of Jackson Monroe."

"It was a little bit of hair."

"You think so?" he balked. "This is a serious matter. I am a naked man standing before you!"

"Why, land sakes, I've never heard of such a thing!"

Jackson and Emaline shifted their attention to the woman in the hallway.

"Aunt Verna," Emaline gasped in surprise. "How long have you been standing there?"

"Just long enough!" The middle-aged woman in a flowing floral dress planted her hands on her hips, outlining her plump hourglass figure. Though her reddish-brown hair was still wound in tiny pink rollers, Jackson was certain she was already dressed for a day's work in the greenhouse out back. He initiated a smile in her direction, but her padded round face remained stern, her small dark eyes full of reproach. The only full-blooded Gypsy in the household was boiling mad.

"The 'naked' remark was a figure of speech," Jackson explained. He had stepped away from the stairs at the sound of her bellow, and was now standing alone in the center of the alcove. Stripped of his shirt, he knew he must look a bit wild. But this woman had seen his bare chest many a time. Probably saw a lot more during his convalescence. She had every right to be shocked and annoyed by his sudden reappearance. But she actually seemed . . . mystified and horrified.

Verna Holt took a step nearer, her heavy chin creasing in two as she studied the towering man from head to toe.

Of course! Aunt Verna didn't view him as a deserter, but as a goner. She naturally believed he'd passed on. He shot Emaline a sharp look. This was Emaline's fault. She deserved this mess dropped in her lap.

"He was speaking of his naked soul," Emaline hastened to explain.

"My naked face, Aunt Verna," Jackson corrected with fiendish pleasure, rocking on his heels.

"The face of his soul," Emaline pounced in again. "His very, very naked soul."

Verna was wagging a puffy finger at him now. "You called me Aunt Verna. You—"

"You are Aunt Verna," Emaline swiftly interceded, wringing her hands.

"Hush, *posh*," Aunt Verna directed, addressing Emaline with an endearment signifying her half-Gypsy heritage. She folded her arms across her ample bosom, eyeing Jackson with wariness. "Explain this mass of confusion, sir."

"I believe I'll allow Emaline to do that," he invited with a small elegant bow and sweep of his huge workman's hand.

"Very well," Emaline assented, inhaling shakily. "Aunt Verna, may I present—"

"Don't tell me, Emaline," she boomed suddenly, catching the pair off balance. "Let me guess."

"No, Auntie," Emaline cringed in panic. "Don't do that."

"Do let her guess, Emaline," Jackson coaxed in petty anticipation. Emaline was caught in a snare of her own lies. Where she belonged!

Verna moved into the alcove and began to circle her prey. "You surely look like a Monroe," she chortled. "Still . . ."

Look like a Monroe? Jackson shrugged uneasily under her scrutiny. Had the woman gone daft—dafter? It was he, the one and only Jackson Monroe. He hadn't changed dramatically in the past several months. True, his beloved beard was gone. But that wasn't enough to put a man's whole identity in question!

This was utterly ridiculous. Watching Emaline squirm and confess would've been a lark, but his honest nature drove him to the point of announcement. "Aunt Verna," he began with a sigh. "Rumors of Jackson's demise—"

"Rumors of Jackson's demise," Emaline swiftly interceded, "didn't reach his brother John until this week."

"Huh?" Jackson did a double take at Emaline, his jaw sagging in befuddlement. She was truly serious!

Aunt Verna would've noticed Jackson's reaction if she hadn't been preparing to take credit for the discovery herself. "I knew it, Emaline," she proclaimed triumphantly. "I knew it was something of the kind. A truly remarkable resemblance. Not twins, of course . . ."

Not twins with himself? How could Verna not recognize him? How could Emaline simply not own up to the truth she had with Lindy last night? Verna continued to slowly circle him, dark eyes snapping with excitement. Jackson turned with her. She was completely mesmerized, studying him as he studied her. How could she not know him?

Suddenly all became clear. Verna's circle brought her past the coat tree, past the front door and then past the ornate mirror next to the closet. As she passed by the mirror, Jackson looked over her shoulder and saw his own reflection in the glass. No wonder Verna didn't know him. Jackson barely recognized himself with his new head of brown hair. Auburn hair to be exact, the reddish, rather garish shade of Verna's!

Emaline had not only shaved his beard, but she'd tinted his hair with her aunt's dye! The twin heads in the reflection were the identical shade!

"Yes," Verna patted a finger against her doughy cheek. "On some levels the resemblance is truly remarkable. But John," she confided in a giddy gush, "I must say, you are the handsomer Monroe. I imagine you heard that all the time as a youngster. Your gray eyes have a silvery twinkle. Your jawline is far stronger. Your hair, too, is . . . definitely more appealing. Longer in style, richer in color. Not that I had anything against Jackson," she assured him with a charming laugh.

Nothing against Jackson? Verna hated Jackson's guts, had since he shifted from Emaline's patient to her suitor. He rubbed his eyes with a groan. It was all a dream, wasn't it? No, if it had been a dream of his making, he'd never have settled for a prebreakfast nipple nudge. He'd have gotten the whole girl last night. No question, he was back in the loony bin he'd once called home.

"I want you to feel completely at home here with us," Verna was saying as he plugged back into the conversation. He must've had his eyes closed for a while, for she now had his shirt in her hand. "You slip this on and we'll have some breakfast. It'll be such fun getting acquainted." With a cheerful hum, she moved down the hallway. "Margaret, Margaret," she called in the distance. "You'll never guess what, dear. We have an unexpected visitor. No surprise really, considering that my eyebrows itched yesterday."

Jackson stole an ominous look at his bride, still hovering near the stairs. "Anything itchin' you?"

"The soles of my feet, actually," Emaline replied, glancing down at her peach ballet slippers. "A clear sign that I'll soon be treading on strange ground."

"You have no idea," he threatened.

"Now, John, I can explain everything," she placated as he advanced.

"John?" he repeated murderously.

"Don't you like the name John?" she asked with genuine concern.

"It's dandy," he growled, jerking one arm, then the other, into the sleeves of his blue cotton work shirt. "For a man who needs one. I didn't need fixin' Emaline. No shave, no dye, no new name!"

"Be patient for a little while," she coaxed, doing up his white plastic buttons. "Until we get used to you all over again."

"Blasted lies!" Jackson inhaled sharply as the tips of her fingernails grazed the hair-dusted line along his sternum. Working at the Tip Top was no doubt the reason her painted nails weren't as long or sharp as they used to be. But he could still imagine the rounded points flicking in and out of his navel, down along the tender skin of his inner thighs.

"Please play along, sweet baby," she pleaded.

Oh, how he melted when she called him that! "Okay, okay, just for now. But you straighten this out, you hear?"

SATURDAY MORNING breakfast was still served in the dining room on the huge cherrywood table covered with snowy linen. Next door neighbor Colin Sinclair was already seated at the head, still obviously an honored Saturday morning guest. Not that Colin didn't drop in during the week, as well, for impromptu dinners and lunches served at the old Formica-topped table in the kitchen. Jackson recalled that Colin was quite available with his flexible work schedule. A British author of children's books, he'd settled in Hollow Tree Junction two years ago with a wish to withdraw from the London hustle and bustle. The creator of two popular series centered around lovable animals with human characteristics—Professor Pigeon, the transatlantic teacher with his own transportation, and Deputy Elephant, a lawphant with a keen nose for sniffing out criminals—he seemed to have plenty of time to visit with the Holts.

Colin never seemed to tire of talking about his Professor and Deputy, even though each series was completed before Jackson's move to Hollow Tree. Despite his claim to be developing bigger and better projects, Colin seemed to be living on past glory and trickling royalties, even cutting his own hair. He was always so present, so available, so interested in the town gossip. Jackson wondered just which lady lit his fire—his mother-in-law, Margaret, or Aunt Verna. Maybe it was only the regular feedings that brought him back again and again.

"See, Colin, I told you so!" Verna exulted, thrusting a finger at Jackson. "Jackson Monroe does indeed have kin. Here is his brother John!" Verna was as animated as a child in the author's presence, her pink rollers miraculously missing, her voice flirtatious and smug. She had a penchant for being in the right.

Colin raised a gray brow, regarding the newcomer from his honored seat. "Could've sworn I was seeing Jackson himself."

"This is John, Colin," Emaline interjected lightly. "John, this is Colin Sinclair, our next-door neighbor."

"Pleasure, John," Colin said airily, far more interested in dipping the corner of his toast into the yolk of his egg.

"Likewise," Jackson returned shortly, grinning as he spied Verna's rollers behind a pot of African violets on the windowsill. He slipped into one of the cherry high-back chairs, discovering that his appetite was returning. Colin's lukewarm reception didn't bother him in the slightest. It was Margaret Holt, Emaline's staid mother, who would be the one to deal with.

A moment later, Margaret glided through the swinging kitchen door dressed in gray slacks and sweater, carrying a pitcher of orange juice. She nearly dropped it at the sight of Jackson, seated beside Emaline. The last man she probably cared to see was another Monroe, blond or auburn.

"Allow me, m'dear," Colin eloquently interceded, rising in a fluid motion to take the juice from Margaret's jittery hands.

"Thank you," Margaret said rather helplessly, her green eyes round as she seated herself beside Colin. "So Verna was not mistaken. Welcome to our home, John."

Jackson smiled at his mother-in-law. He had always liked Margaret, though she'd so vehemently opposed his marriage to Emaline. She was a cautious woman by nature, who found him totally unacceptable as a husband for her daughter.

"Why, John, it seems you have many of Jackson's tastes," Aunt Verna broke in excitedly, disrupting Jackson's train of thought.

"Lots of people like their eggs sunny-side up, Auntie," Lindy said with a playful giggle, sliding into the last empty chair beside her mother.

"Still, it's so remarkable that Jackson has a brother who so resembles him," Verna pressed on dramatically. "Like two different shades of mums growing on the same plant. Pink and white," she added for visual effect.

"Speaking of plants, has anyone seen the new seed catalog that came in the mail yesterday?" Margaret asked, spreading a thin layer of jam on her toast.

"I guess I have, Mother," Lindy confessed, grinning impishly.

"You, Lindy?" Verna queried, aghast. "Don't tell me you're finally going to take an interest in the greenhouse."

"Gee, no, Auntie," Lindy scoffed, reaching for the pitcher of juice. "My dressing table upstairs is a little wobbly, so I put the catalog under the shorter leg."

"You bring that catalog back right after breakfast," Margaret directed patiently.

Jackson watched Margaret rise to round the table with a steeping pot of tea. Always the proper hostess. Just as dark, lanky, Lindy apparently favored her missing father, Emaline looked very much like her fair German mother. Both shared the thick mane of light hair, rounded hips that swayed with every step. Both of them had exotically tilted eyes, Margaret's a forthright green, Emaline's a mysterious black.

Jackson focused on his plate as Margaret caught him staring. He understood the wariness he found in her gimlet gaze. After being deserted herself, naturally she'd hoped Emaline would connect with a small-town fellow with roots. She wondered about his intentions. Was he just another handy Monroe like his brother?

"Yes, John," Verna continued in a loud, bell-like voice. "Jackson was greatly admired around here during his sojourn under our roof. First the accident, then the marriage. He was here almost a year, actually."

"Not quite, Verna," Margaret corrected automatically.

"Yes," Verna murmured, ignoring her sister-in-law. "He was well liked, indeed, especially by me. He and I had a special tie."

A special tie? Nothing less than a hangman's noose, perhaps. Jackson inhaled sharply, a piece of egg lodging in his windpipe. He coughed uncontrollably.

"John!" Emaline reached over and slapped him hard on the back. He swallowed, his watering eyes glazing in disbelief.

"Jackson was cherished by all of us," Emaline affirmed, rubbing the length of his spine. "Another pea in our happy little pod." She gave him a final pat and returned to her food.

"Can I get you anything?" Margaret asked not unkindly, setting the china pot back on the sideboard.

"No, thanks," he replied numbly.

"It's a cryin' shame you had to miss your brother's funeral," Lindy broke in with feigned remorse, her dark eyes glinting playfully behind her sweeping black lashes.

"You certainly must've been out of touch to miss out on his demise," Verna clucked sympathetically.

"It can happen," Emaline jumped in. "Why, relatives lose touch every day. And never touch again," she added with a significant lilt to her tone.

Jackson stole a glance at Emaline. She deliberately avoided his eyes, busily stirring a pool of cream into her coffee. The message was clear. If he blew the whistle on her now, he'd be losing touch with her permanently. And oh, how he wanted to touch her!

"I, ah, lost contact with Jackson around the time he settled here, I suppose," he lied with a mournful tone fueled by his surging libido. "Naturally, I had no idea that he'd married, or died." He bowed his head for a moment of meditation. His eyes wrinkled shut and his mouth curved slightly, as if he were willing himself to relive a memory he'd shared with his late brother. He was actually thinking of how much satisfaction he'd get from taking his bride over his knee for a sound swatting.

"We understood that Jackson had no family." Margaret's soft, maternal words tamed his wild angry visions.

"Just brother and me." Jackson lifted his head, bestowing a rueful smile on his mother-in-law.

"John's a lawyer!" Lindy joyously expounded. "He's got a steady job in Ohio and everything."

Lindy's announcement drew murmurs of approval and surprise around the table. Jackson glared at her in warning. But it was too late—another stone had been mounted on the house of lies. Jackson could tell by her hopeful expression, that she had his best interest at heart. Jackson the carpenter, drifting from town to town to ply his trade, had not been considered the ideal mate for Emaline in Margaret's and Verna's eyes. But John the lawyer might fare pretty well.

"You have your own practice, John?" Margaret asked, brightening considerably.

"That's right, Mother," Emaline assured her.

"Wills, banking, murders," Lindy babbled on. "All kinds of neat stuff."

"How did you track Jackson to Hollow Tree Junction?" Colin asked.

"Apparently one of Jackson's letters caught up with John in Ohio," Emaline hastily intervened, nibbling nervously on a slice of bacon. "It seems John was in New York for many years. Jackson didn't know he'd relocated. Anyway, John, ah, sent Jackson a telegram here about twelve days ago." Before they could protest too loudly, she forged on. "I didn't tell any of you, because I didn't know a thing about John. I sent him back a telegram, explaining the situation. And he . . . just showed up," she finished awkwardly.

"Must've been an incredible shock to you," Verna clucked sympathetically. "Finding out Jackson passed on."

"Quite frankly, I was astounded."

"I was the first to greet him, comfort him," Lindy chirped, winding some strands of kinky black hair around her finger. "There he was, standing in the doorway, his hat in his hand."

The little sadist! Jackson frowned as Lindy winked at him. If Margaret ever found out her little girl had found him in the tub, he might very well end up in the cemetery before his time!

"Of course Emaline never would've buried Jackson without your instructions, John," Margaret consoled him. "Had we known . . ."

"Jackson and I weren't particularly close," Jackson told her, fumbling for explanations. He could barely believe he was participating in Emaline's charade. But one look her way was reminder enough. She was absolutely alluring, her small chin lifted in false bravado, her full lower lip ripe in a pout. But the onyx eyes told the true story—the vulnerability, the desperation. A wife was supposed to tug at a man's strings, he knew. But blast it all, she had no right to yank them out of his heart!

He took a sip of tea, his mind racing. He knew the moment his expression had shifted to mischievous, for Emaline blanched under her pink powdered cheeks. Perhaps he would extract some pleasures of his own from all of this muddle.

"So, just how did my brother meet his demise?" He asked soberly, steepling his fingers to hide his growing smirk.

"A hero's death!" Verna proclaimed, her voice regal. "The man is a saint, sir. A saint living right in here in the comfort of my bosom for all time." She dropped her eyes in respect, softly beating her chest three times with a closed fist.

Jackson's hands fell from his flabbergasted face as he focused on Verna's heaving knockers, threatening to burst forth from the V neckline of her dress. He was trapped in there?

Verna nodded sagely, her fleshy chin quivering. "Is it all so hard to believe, John?" she asked, questioning his open scowl of disbelief.

"Well," he gulped. "Jackson has never before been called a . . . a—"

4

"A SAINT!"

"A hero!"

"A prince of a fella," Emaline chimed in after her aunt and sister. She forced herself to turn to Jackson at her right. He seared her soul with his sidelong look of disbelief, distrust. She wanted to tell him so many things, especially that she'd tossed and turned the night away wondering just how to handle this very moment. It would no doubt seem so complicated to him, but it was actually very simple. And who should know the details better than she, the widow of Jackson Monroe?

"Is it so hard to believe, John?" Verna implored, her eyes glistening. "Surely as his kin, you know firsthand of Jackson's sterling qualities?"

Verna pulled a lacy kerchief from the very bosom where he now apparently lived, dabbing her damp lashes with an emotional sniffle. He considered himself a decent guy... but a blasted saint? He scanned the table, looking for a sign of opposition. Incredibly, no one leaped to argue the issue. "Tell me how it all happened," he requested dazedly.

"Jackson died saving the life of another," Emaline reported wistfully. "You see, he was working on a construction site in Norfolk—"

"Trying to save money so he and Emaline could build their dream cottage," Lindy tossed in eagerly, scoping the group for their reaction to her latest fabrication.

"You never told us that, Emaline." Margaret broke in. "I thought you and Jackson were content with the third-floor suite."

Darn that Lindy! She'd soon spoil a perfectly good tale. Emaline shot little sister an admonishing look.

"Barmy," Colin agreed, stroking his narrow jawline. "Jackson worked like a madman on that old bedroom attic of yours, Emaline. Why would he suddenly change course and think of moving out?"

"That strip of property down by Miller Creek is pretty spectacular," Lindy expounded joyously.

"Lindy Holt!" Emaline cut in sharply. "Jackson worked in Norfolk to fortify our nest egg. He and I had no particular plans! Remember?" she prodded in thinly veiled warning.

"Sure, sure, now I remember," Lindy conceded, digging her fork into her fried potatoes.

"So, did he save a fellow construction worker?" Jackson asked brightly, finding himself keen for details of his derring-do.

"Better," Aunt Verna blissfully cooed with the wave of a plump bejeweled hand. She bent over in her chair, scooping up a bundle of white fur. "This, John, is Puff-Puff."

"Huh?" Jackson blinked in confusion at the small, mewing cat curling up against the bosom where he now apparently lived.

"Jackson died saving Puff-Puff," Emaline verified brightly, patting Jackson's hand on the pristine table-cloth.

"He saved that cat?"

"He darted into traffic after this poor creature," Aunt Verna confirmed, lovingly stroking her furry friend. "Without a thought to his own safety, mind you. Thank goodness Emaline wasn't on hand to witness the accident. She just happened to be in town that very day, planning to visit Jackson at the construction site. Imagine fate's heavy hand in this whole episode!" Aunt Verna obviously paused to do just that, her lower lip quivering. "By the time Emaline got there, the tragedy itself was blessedly over. The truck had moved, and the remains of Jackson Monroe were in an ambulance."

"How fortunate for you, Emaline, to miss the remains." Jackson's voice was brittle as he slipped his hand out from under her nervous pats of comfort.

"I did what I had to do," Emaline said, tilting her pert chin with a ragged sigh. And the truth did indeed mingle with the fabrications. If only she could count on Jackson to distinguish the differences, and appreciate that she'd enhanced his memory!

"Puff-Puff rose like a phoenix from the depths of tragedy," Aunt Verna proclaimed fervently. "It was *Romany kushti bok*."

"That's 'good luck' to non-Gypsy gaujos like you and me, John," Margaret explained, nibbling on her toast.

"And me," Colin chimed in, reaching for the last muffin in the basket on the table.

Verna inhaled, venturing to philosophize. "Puff-Puff was a loner off the streets, just as Jackson once was. Jackson obviously wanted him to find his way to our home. He willed it from beyond," she trailed off with a sweeping gesture.

From beyond the bathtub.

Jackson grimaced as Lindy raised a glass of water to him, tipping it back and forth so the clear liquid crested and splashed over the rim, trickling down her ringed fingers.

"How careless of you, Lindy," Margaret scolded, reaching over to dab the damp tablecloth with her napkin.

Lindy dimpled impishly. "Too much sloshing can make a mess."

Another woman child in the family, Jackson groaned inwardly. Lindy had been just a kid last summer.

"It seemed like a shame not to bring the kitty back with me," Emaline said, steering the conversation back to his heroism. "I did feel a strong inkling the moment I picked up Puff-Puff." She tossed her aunt a smile, causing the plump woman to glow.

"That is hard to imagine," Jackson bit out.

"We have a spiritual connection to all creatures," Verna said, her dark eyes gleaming. "You may not believe it, but I actually nurture our plants in the greenhouse with love and respect as well as water and sunlight."

Oh, he believed it, all right! The plants were given far more respect than Jackson Monroe!

Verna's auburn head bobbed with certainty. "If Jackson's last wish was to leave a legacy for us, he chose the perfect vessel."

"Jackson and I are linked till the end of time, John," Emaline explained. "No matter how far away he is, I can still feel him."

Jackson shot her a knavish smile. "Feel him, eh?"

"Why, yes." Emaline gasped as Jackson's hand suddenly crept into her lap beneath the hem of the tablecloth. Oh, how she could feel him now! He was furious with her and still desired her. Keeping him from claiming his husbandly rights was going to be difficult. But absolutely necessary. At least for the time being.

"We really must read John's tea leaves," Verna declared abruptly. She rose from her chair, set Puff-Puff on Colin's lap and bustled round the table.

"Perhaps another time, Auntie," Emaline protested, stiffening in her seat as Jackson's hand inched up her thigh, squeezing, kneading her through the erotically slippery satin of her gown.

"Let the poor stiff be," Colin reproved, setting the cat on the floor. If his words had a double meaning, he didn't reveal so in his manner.

"I don't mind at all," Jackson intoned, using his free right hand to clasp Verna's as she hovered at his side. She was so involved in her fortune-telling that she didn't even notice the absence of his left one from the table. The hand that was so busy entertaining Emaline.

"I shall tell you what to do, dear," Verna declared excitedly.

"All right," he said with a benign smile.

Verna released her grip on him, gesturing to the cup and saucer. "Now, sip down just a dribble more tea. Good. Keep hold of the handle. A little more."

"I'm trying," he assured her with a winsome smile.

Emaline's sweeping golden lashes shaded the flame now burning deeply within her dark eyes. His hot fingers were clenching, demanding, cutting through the folds of her gown like knives in soft butter. Jolts of passion electrified her system, making her quiver with desire. There was no whimsy to his touch—he wanted her with urgency. There were ways to overcome clever stalls, lies and alibis. He was proving it under all of their noses! Didn't he realize that he'd already left a burning impression on her heart, which would linger for all time?

"John, I need your left hand now," Verna directed as he drained his tea nearly to the bottom of the white china cup.

"Yes, John," Emaline agreed, giving his hand a sharp nudge off her lap. "You wanted to do this, so do it."

"Very well."

Emaline released a weak sigh of relief as the sweet five-finger torment withdrew itself. But as for the fortune . . .

"Rotate the cup three times," Verna continued. "That's it. Clockwise. Swirl those leaves around, up to the rim, too. Now, tip the cup upside down in your saucer. Excellent. Now make a wish."

A slow, languid smile spread over Jackson's face as he lowered his lids and did as instructed. Emaline winced as he eventually opened his eyes, turning to her with a gloating grin. He didn't believe in these rituals, but they both knew she did. She could only imagine what he'd wished for!

"Now for the cup . . ." Verna began, only to have Emaline snatch it from the saucer. "What are you doing, *posh?*"

"John's reading." Holding the cup close to her chest, she scanned the swirling leaf patterns inside with an educated eye.

"Let me see," Verna impatiently ordered, thrusting a fleshy arm across Jackson's line of vision.

"He is my brother-in-law," Emaline argued, tipping back in her chair.

"He is my nephew-in-law," Verna chortled. "Kin to the man who lives within my heart." With a powerful swipe, she snatched the cup from Emaline. "Why, it makes no sense at all," she paused to judge in frustration. "There should be circles, not broken lines."

"Circles stand for completion, John," Lindy offered, alight with dimpled amusement. "Broken lines mean broken promises."

"Totally absurd," huffed Verna. "And what is this near the bottom?"

"Truly nothing," Emaline counted, a frantic note in her light voice.

"'Tis a boomerang," Verna judged in annoyance. "Now what would a dear man like John know of retributive justice?"

"You are about to gather the fruits of your own actions," Lindy recited with pleasure. "That is the boomerang symbol."

"A boomerang is something thrown great distances only to turn in midflight and return, is it not?" Colin asked, shoveling a forkful of diced cantaloupe into his mouth. During the ruckus, he'd returned to the sideboard for a fresh plate of food.

"There is a scissors, too. People working at cross-purposes? Perhaps we need the cards," Verna suggested. "Or the crystal. Surely John will be staying on with us for a time so we can probe further."

"Yes, John, you must," Margaret agreed. "I only wish we had a guest room. If Colin weren't in the middle of a grueling project, perhaps he could've taken our John in." Despite her ready excuse for her neighbor, Margaret managed to put Colin on the spot with her subtle, beguiling approach.

"Sorry, Margaret, love," Colin intoned, his final bites ingested with opportune speed and timing. "I suggest you clear out the pantry as you did for Jackson. He was quite cozy in there the weeks before his wedding."

"Oh, the pantry will be perfect for John," Aunt Verna put in, nuzzling her face in Puff-Puff's fur.

Jackson remembered the postage-stamp room holding shelves of canned goods. If you'd asked him about bunking there yesterday as he covered mile after mile on his Harley, he'd have hooted in your face. He belonged upstairs, in his bed! He was more flexible today, however. He desperately needed that space to lay his head. He couldn't bear to be put out now. The only way to wear Emaline down was with relentless persuasion. If he failed, John could just as well join his brother over yonder, leaving a puppy behind in his place.

"We can rearrange some of the things in there," Margaret assured him, "to accommodate the foldaway bed."

Colin dabbed his mouth with his snowy napkin and rose. "On that cheery note, I must take leave," he announced smoothly, palming an apple as he paused by the sideboard. "I have some muse work to do. And I'm sure John can maneuver quite handily without assistance."

"Perhaps you'd like another cup of tea, Colin," Aunt Verna broke in, her face clouding as he dropped his napkin on the table. "There's nearly an entire cup of milk here just for you."

"As much as I appreciate your gesture of supplying me with my own cream and sugar set, dear Verna, I must decline. Take heed, there's always tomorrow. Ta-ta." With a wave, the thin, lanky man breezed through the kitchen doorway.

"There's always lunch today," Lindy said snidely as the back screen door snapped shut in the distance. "There's high tea, low tea, afternappy-time tea."

"We want Colin to come, don't we, Margaret?" Aunt Verna implored her sister-in-law.

"Of course, Verna," Margaret agreed. "And we want you, John," she added, bestowing a warm smile on Jackson.

It was a smile he'd only observed many times before. Margaret's soft green eyes crinkled just a little at the corners, her face lifted just a fraction. It felt satisfying to have the smile bestowed on him for once.

The gut feeling was a shock. Was he softening as he approached the thirty-year mark? He'd never cared much what people thought of him before. Handyman Jackson had always neatly loosened binding ties and fled before the knots tightened in suffocation. It was so unlike him to care what these women thought of him. So unlike him to return to a sticky situation.

If only he could make Emaline see what it had taken for him to come back to Hollow Tree for her! He deserved a hero's welcome as the genuine Jackson Monroe. At least from his Emaline. He loved her till it hurt. Making her understand was going to be a far greater challenge than he'd ever dreamed. If only he could get her into a bed, even that rickety foldaway. He'd prove his love. He'd prove it so thoroughly that they'd have to retire that old bed to the junk heap, or to a museum. The decision would be Emaline's.

"FRESH SHEETS for the boomerang boy!"

Jackson spun on his boot heel at Lindy's proclamation, watching as she waltzed into the pantry with an armload of linens. Emaline followed with a freestanding mirror. Both sisters were dressed in jeans and pastel blouses, Lindy's pink, Emaline's mint. Both had their long, thick hair secured in a ponytail, Lindy's ebony, Emaline's corn silk.

Partners in crime and in cleanup. For an hour, the entire family had worked on the whitewashed storage room off the kitchen, shifting boxes and canned goods, vacuuming, dusting. Not only was there space for the foldaway bed, but also for a tall, narrow highboy that Margaret had ferreted out of Colin's garage under the neighbor's vague, doleful eye. Lindy had lagged behind Colin's unkempt hedge, producing a triumphant smile and an old wagon when Colin challenged them on just how they would transport the dresser across the wide expanse of lawn between the houses.

"Stop calling me boomerang."

"But if the boom fits," she whined.

"Drop the boom, and the sheets on the bed, please, Lindy," Emaline instructed as she adjusted the mirror atop the varnished pine dresser.

"Ah, a mirror," Jackson said, clasping his hands together in abandon. "How lovely."

"Just what you need to remind yourself of who you are now," Lindy said with glee.

"I need a psychiatrist for that undertaking," he snorted skeptically, yanking open his knapsack on the wobbly wicker chair in the corner. He dug through the last of his belongings, joining Emaline at the dresser to toss some T-shirts and socks into the top drawer. The scent of her fragrant shampoo assailed his nostrils as he hovered over her head. He'd been as jumpy as a tiger the entire hour, waiting for the others to leave. He needed answers almost as much as he needed her. Almost as much.

Emaline whirled on him suddenly, her long ponytail swiping his throat like a strip of luxuriant sable.

"Maybe you better get out of here, kid," he gruffly suggested to Lindy as a rough shudder shook him in his boots.

"Yes, Lindy," Emaline agreed, to his surprise. "But before you do . . ." She'd obviously spied something in Jackson's knapsack. She crossed the room, withdrawing a box of cigars. "Better take these with you."

"What!" Jackson thundered, stomping between the females to rescue his precious stogies. "They don't sell anything like that here at the drugstore. I picked those up in Manhattan. At a little place near Battery Park."

"Mother expressed concerned that you might be a smoker, too—"

"Too?" he repeated, his jaw tightening.

"As Jackson was," she clarified with an impatient huff.

"I see."

"Anyway, she didn't want to see the pantry smoked up, so..." Emaline trained off, her creamy slender hands aflutter.

"So I'll smoke on the porch," he negotiated reasonably.

"Sorry, John, but I told her you didn't smoke at all."

"Blasted damnation!" he roared in outrage, shaking a clenched fist.

"We all truly hated those cigars," Emaline confided, patting him gently on the shoulder.

"Get out, Lindy," he ordered, grabbing hold of Emaline's ponytail before she could step away. When Lindy paused for instructions from her mentor, Jackson jerked a thumb at the doorway. "Leave without Emaline, and without my cigars. And close the door behind you!"

When Emaline nodded, Lindy meekly slipped out.

"Close it tight!" A moment or two passed before the lock clicked in place. "That kid!" he fumed, releasing Emaline's hair with a flourish. "And you, wife!"

"Are there codes about cigars, too?" she asked evenly, her dark eyes snapping.

"There oughta be!" He paced the room, tossing the box back in his sack. "Do you realize you are methodically stripping me of every creature pleasure I cherish?" he spat despairingly. "Whiskers, smokes, the very hair on my head! And there isn't even any sex in it for me! I may just lose the will to live. But what the hell, I'm supposed to be deceased, anyway!"

"It's all part of the big picture, John. But I suppose you want me to apologize. Apologize for making you a hero in the eyes of the town, for saving—" She caught her breath in midsentence, inwardly debating whether to continue. "Oh, never mind!" she eventually cried. She reached for the bottom sheet on the bed, snapping it open across the mattress.

Jackson frowned in confusion. For saving what? Blasted Puff-Puff? "You will not twist this around, wife," he warned, prowling round the rickety rollaway. "It's your pride that's fueled you. It's your pride you must swallow."

Clenching the sheet, she whirled on him in fury. "I couldn't let them think just anything. Not about you, my husband. I really did go to Norfolk. On the bus. I went to Norfolk and brought Verna back the kind of kitty she's always wanted, and a coffin full of rocks just for you."

"But why the pretense, wife?" He tore the sheet from her fumbling hands and tossed it back on the mattress.

"Because the funeral home in Eagle Point is too close for comfort, that's why," she replied with strained patience. "You know we don't have our own here and folks from there talk to the folks here all the time. Somebody would've found out about the rocks and spilled the whole deal. Don't you see? They don't give a hoot about lies in a big city like Norfolk. I could've bought an even dozen boxes without anybody batting an eye. Filled 'em with whipped cream, too, just as long as I was willing to pay." She stopped short, breathless.

"Emaline, how can I make you understand?" He squeezed his eyes shut for a second, searching for the proper words. "A man . . . a man has an ego, an inner machismo."

"Like pride?" she asked crisply, folding her arms across her chest.

"Well, uh, yeah," he conceded, watching her eyes glimmer with triumph. "But it's different. It's simply has to do with being a man. Men understand it."

"Like the codes, I suppose."

"Yes! It's all woven together in this intricate masculine mystique thing," he explained.

"Pride, John," she clucked. "Simple pride."

Jackson moved closer, gritting his teeth in frustration. "What I am trying to say, wife, is . . . What I mean is . . . If you were going all the way to Norfolk, anyway, why couldn't I have saved a human life? You know, like a fellow worker, or a little old lady crossing under a girder, a waif selling flowers on a street corner to pay for her pa's operation? As long as you were making it up and all . . ." Jackson knew the issue was senseless, but the question was a symbol of all his frustration rolled up into one white fur ball.

"Saving Puff-Puff was a noble thing to do," Emaline soothed, running a hand over his furrowed forehead. She should've colored his brows, too, she fleetingly realized. Maybe next time . . . No, it was too late for touch-ups. They knew John as he was today. And they accepted him golden browed and all. They accepted John as she'd wished they'd accepted Jackson. That ache, along with others, throbbed on with the passion.

"I just don't get it," he growled.

"I did the best I could," she told him bleakly. "It was sleeting when I got to Norfolk on that bleak February morning. I looked for a place to stay, found a nice coffin for you. Then I wandered around downtown for a while, deciding just what story to tell everybody. Of course I had that one thin shred of hope . . ." she trailed off feebly.

"What hope?" he demanded. "That you'd find a replacement?"

"That I'd find you there in Norfolk," she confessed with a cry. "That you'd want us back."

She'd looked for him in Norfolk.

Emaline's admission was gut wrenching. He'd been hundreds of miles away from Nebraska by then. Guilt and remorse engulfed Jackson. He seized her shoulders with the nonsensical fear that she might evaporate. The fact that it was he, not Emaline, who did the evaporating in the first place didn't calm him any. He couldn't bear to lose her again.

Emaline's heart turned over as Jackson drew her close, trapping her between the bed and his solid chest. She could sense his urgency, read his mind as surely as if she were gazing into the crystal. She forced herself to continue calmly, to keep her cool above all else.

"I happened to pass a pet shop and spotted Puff-Puff behind a wall of glass," she continued. "Naturally, she didn't have a name yet. But I looked that kitty in the eye and I knew she was the answer to all of my problems. Mother could've swayed either way, but Aunt Verna values animals far above most humans. Your saving Puff-Puff was most gallant of gestures." She rested a reassuring hand on his shoulder. "It's been so wonderful to finally hear them sing the praises of my Jackson Monroe."

"You have to tell them the truth," he coerced.

"I cannot do so," she argued, aware that his arms had tightened considerably around her middle, that the rail of the bed frame was digging into the back of her legs.

"I say you were wrong to spin such tales. I hate lies. I think you should've handled this whole thing better, given me a way back home." His voice softened a fraction. "Didn't it ever occur to you, my sweet, innocent darling, that you are a totally irresistible woman? That your husband couldn't stay away forever?"

"No!" Her admission was laced with regret. "I did the very best I could. I thought long and hard before going to Norfolk, getting the kitty. Though saving a human life sounds more heroic, I would have had to bring that human back to Hollow Tree for inspection. What sort of a person lets you sacrifice your life, then has the nerve to skip your funeral?"

An agonizing moan surged from his throat. Good lord, she was making sense!

"Just what I would've needed," she fumed, "a second body I couldn't produce!"

Jackson's mind was spinning like a funnel cloud, picking up all sorts of useless things in its touchdowns to earth. There were many, many answers to ferret out. Yes, Emaline was full of explanation, but she was quite selective, obviously telling him only what she pleased. "You should've told the truth then, you should tell the truth right now!" he insisted. No matter what she was concealing, overall honesty would've been the right course of action.

"And have you take off on me again?" she said, aghast. "They'd never believe me a second time, not without a real body, anyway!"

"But I'll never leave you again, I promise."

"You made all sorts of promises the first time," she reproved.

"I am a different man now."

"Thanks to me!"

"Yes, thanks to you, Emaline. But not in the way you think. I've come to realize that we need time to nurture our love, time to work at ironing out the rough spots. I had to leave you to realize I couldn't live without you. The changes happened inside my head, not on top of it," he claimed, ruffling his dyed hair.

"Don't try to confuse me, John, it isn't fair!"

"Confuse you, wife?" he uttered in shock. "I'm the one who's floating in a sea of loneliness, total bewilderment. And that's not even counting my whole new identity as some boring conservative lawyer." He shook his head. "Don't try and deny it, Emaline, you've always had a bewitching way about you with all of your spells and incantations. I don't believe you can draw upon the powers of the universe, but drawing on my energies," he finished rather uncertainly, "that you seem quite adept at." He searched her eyes, looking for a glimmer of understanding. "Can I get through to you still? Have I ever gotten through?"

If only he knew just what an effect he was having on her at that very moment. Emaline groaned inwardly, leaning into him as her knees quaked. It felt so good to be in his arms, pinned against him with last night's intimacy without the untamed rage.

This was the man she loved.

Emaline undid her ponytail, shaking her hair loose. Her hands were on the loose, as well, moving anxiously over the broad expanse of his chest, feeling the familiar valleys, hard, muscled surfaces beneath the cotton of his blue shirt. This was the body that had taught her about physical pleasure, entering her, exploring her, consuming her whole over and over again. She closed her eyes to focus on past passions, inhaling in short nervous jerks, appreciating his masculine scent as if it were the last traces of life-giving oxygen in a raging fire.

But Jackson was the fire as well as the air. Jackson was the cause and the cure! Flames licked her insides red-hot, and he was quenching them with the familiar tenderness. The soft whisper of her name at her ear, the pressure of a moist kiss at her throat. The ultimate safety she felt in his arms. Yes, he would take her to the danger zone, but he would shelter her all the while.

His hands moved greedily along her back, her denim-covered bottom, through her thick corn silk hair. He was cradling her in his arms, easing her back, back to the old striped mattress on the rollaway behind her. It was all a prelude to the journey to the dizzying heights. To the stars . . .

To the moon.

Emaline broke free with a cry of fright, just as he was about to ease her onto the rumpled bed.

"Trust me, Emaline," he pleaded, trying to reach for her as she scrambled behind Colin's dresser.

"I'm sorry, John, I—I can't."

"Don't call me John, dammit," he demanded with a clenched fist. "Not when we're alone. Not when we're about to—" There was agony in his tone, beneath the lion's roar.

"We're not about to do anything," she whimpered, her fragile features mirroring his pain.

"It's no accident that I've come home days before the harvest celebration, sweet Emaline. Don't think for a minute it was fate, or magic, the luck of the draw." The gravity of his words and gaze followed her as she stumbled back a step. "Last year was bountiful for us, remember?" He lifted a rakish brow. "You, me, the blanket. And the full harvest moon itself, of course. We wore nothing but the silvery beams upon our backsides," he mused with reminiscent pleasure. "Seems to me we glowed long after the moon was set."

"You know nothing of the moon, gaujo fool!" Emaline rushed to the door for escape, yanking it open without grace. She scampered across the kitchen and up the back staircase. Jackson didn't follow on foot, but his laugh filled with male determination nipped at her ears long into the afternoon.

5

"Why, Emaline, I thought the swing was creaking in the wind." Margaret Holt stepped out onto the front porch later on Saturday evening, openly surprised to find her daughter pensively gliding back and forth. Still dressed in her jeans and blouse, her hair done up in a ponytail, Emaline looked like a tomboy dreaming of her first date.

"I'm just out here ponderin' things, Mother."

With one hand on the swing chair, Margaret eased onto the bench beside her. "What are you fingering at your throat?"

Emaline swiftly withdrew her hand from the pearly moonstone pendant.

"The stone of dreams, passions of the night!" Margaret reproved mildly. "The one from your father, no doubt."

"Even if you don't believe in its mystical powers, you have to understand it's the last gift he gave me before leaving," Emaline whispered.

Since Margaret didn't believe in any forms of magic, Emaline knew it would start a row if she blurted out the truth. That she was wearing the stone to put herself in harmony with the energies of the moon; that it might be a way to rid herself of the moonstruck curse set upon her marriage and that of her own mother's. She couldn't help but sit out here in fretful meditation. Such rituals were supposed to be started at the first quarter of the moon, and here it was, days before autumnal equinox! Was it too late in the cycle to stop the inevitable tragedy from repeating itself? Most likely. Rituals had to be followed to the precise letter. Still, it was soothing to sit here in the darkness, rubbing the smooth milky-white stone.

As Emaline well knew, the repercussions of the curse had been affecting the Holts for years. Aunt Verna had recounted her parents' downfall over and over again as customary bedtime fare. Willie Holt had left the home front not because of a faulty marriage, but because of the fickle moon! Willie and Margaret had made love under the harvest moon years ago, and Willie had taken off within a matter of weeks.

Emaline should've resisted when Jackson lured her into the open cornfield on the Withers farm last September twenty-third. But she'd gambled that the lovers curse wasn't hereditary.

The moon had always been her ally over the years. Many of the wishes she'd made on this very porch with this very moon had come true. Jackson himself had even taken a shine to its luminescent shine. But he'd soon disappeared, just as her father had fifteen years ago! She'd been too ashamed to tell even Verna what had really happened.

"Where is John?"

"Off on a motorcycle ride." Emaline rolled her head back against the swing to regard her mother with suspicion. "Why?"

Margaret raised a tawny, perplexed brow. "I just thought the two of you would be together, commiserating over your loss. Seems like the chance of a lifetime, considering your mutual link."

She couldn't have said it better herself, Emaline mused. Desire coiled hotly inside her as she recalled their earlier encounter in the pantry. Jackson was a virile man with insatiable hungers, a rapacious appetite for only her. But the gaujo fool had chosen the worst time of the year to return. On the eve of harvest moon, when the silvery sphere lit up the night for hours on end, when the town gathered to sing and dance, and rejoice over their reaped rewards.

The very celebration that he considered to be their good-luck charm had destroyed their happiness last time around. He'd timed his return to coincide with ruin, utter ruin! Emaline would not make love to him again without an antidote to the curse; for if she did, he would surely ramble off again. She would find a cure quickly. Her ache for him was growing more unbearable.

"You look pale, Emaline," Margaret observed, raising a gentle hand to her daughter's temple.

"I'm weary with the happenings of late," Emaline confessed bleakly.

"Finding John on our doorstep has been quite a shock. But such a nice man. I sense a gentility about him beneath all of those muscles. A sensitivity to our female frailties."

A bogus lawyer with a smooth line and infectious boyish charm, that was Jackson-John Monroe! And after one lousy day, Mother was singing his praises. "Jackson was just as sensitive as John seems to be," Emaline blurted out in pent-up frustration.

"Why, yes, Emaline." Margaret faltered awkwardly, studying her blunt colorless nails in the shadows. "I concede you may have a point, especially after the gallant way he saved Puff-Puff. Perhaps our judgment was a trifle stern."

"Perhaps?" she repeated forcefully. "After a measly twenty-four hours you're eager to accept this . . . this brother. My Jackson was here for months. He was the man I loved!"

"If he deserved more of a chance, I can only say it is regrettable," Margaret whispered. "But John is easier for Verna and me to respect. He is an attorney with a steady income and roots. Jackson was a handyman living from one adventure to the next. You can't blame us for thinking that you were just one more of his adventures."

"But you both loved my father!" she argued. "He, too, was a nomad."

"Ah, yes, my wandering Willie," Margaret said forlornly. "His footloose ways and dark Romany features made him mysteriously irresistible in the beginning . . . but it was a mistake to believe he'd ever settle down. I suspected Jackson would follow in his footsteps—to coin a phrase. I was prejudiced against Jackson because of Willie. And I think Verna was, too, despite her love for her brother. We didn't wish to see you abandoned."

"Jackson loved me! I'm more sure of it now than ever!"

"I admit that Jackson didn't abandon you, he passed on. Please don't fault us for fussing over John," Margaret entreated, patting Emaline's shoulder. "Verna and I see him as our second chance with a Monroe, an unexpected gift from out of the blue. You know," she mused, gazing up at the stars, "I believe even our stranger-wary Lindy has taken to John, as if she's known him for ages. A favor she's never extended to Colin."

"Yes, I've noticed her shine for John. She teases him mercilessly, just as she did . . ."

"Jackson had many good points," Margaret recognized. "I just believe that John has more." She rose from the swing, running a hand through her graying hair as she headed for the screen door. "Think about it, Emaline. Sweet dreams."

Alone again, Emaline rubbed her hands over her face, muffling a moan of lament. Oh, what a tangled web! With Lindy's rash assistance, they managed to make John look too good! Would Jackson consider . . . No, it would be too much to ask. Too much to suggest he remain in the role of John forevermore. It was meant to be only a temporary bandage, until all the wounds were healed. He already missed his beard, his blond hair, his stinky stogies. And worst of all, he was just too doggone honest to go through with it.

"MORNIN', BOOMERANG SLEEPYHEAD."

Jackson pivoted on the green-dotted linoleum floor at the sound of the sultry voice in the kitchen doorway.

"Lindy." Disappointed, he realized it was the junior league.

"Seems like you're always let down when it's me." Her pout slowly spread to a coy curve as she scanned the worn jeans riding low on his hips and the white T-shirt stretched across his broad chest.

"What are you starin' at?" he grumbled, rubbing a hand through his tousled hair.

"Nothin' I ain't seen before," she said, giggling. "You gonna shave? Emaline said to ask you. She said—"

"Yes, I'm going to shave," he cut in impatiently. "At least for today. I'm taking one growth at a time, though," he warned, leaning a hip into the counter.

"Sure, Jackie-John, sure." She sidled into the room, snapping up the shade over the sink. "Must've been tired to sleep so late. It's nearly ten! I suppose it's exhaustion, huh? Some kind of jet lag."

"Maybe." Actually Jackson had lain awake on the narrow rollaway for hours, quelling his sexual surges by studying the puzzle of Emaline and the missing money. What happened to the generous monthly allotments intended to keep her comfortable? Was Colin a closet gigolo, siphoning dough out of this place? Could Emaline be paying him in more than eggs and meat to entertain the elder ladies? Could she be so fearful that he'd take off, too, leaving Margaret and Verna without male company?

There was also the Tip Top owner, Milton Dooley, to ponder. Why was Emaline working for him? She knew Dooley put Jackson through hell while he was remodeling the café's back kitchen. Then the fire destroyed his craftsmanship, making the jerk totally unbearable. Why the whole town knew he was a mean skinflint. Jackson just couldn't understand any of it. The extra money should've kept her life straight!

Jackson had been tempted to demand answers yesterday during their tryst in the pantry. But he had wanted to declare his love before drilling her about practicalities. He shook his head. Would the time ever be right for plain straight talk in this house?

"I'm going to have some of that jet lag someday." Lindy was rambling on dreamily, twirling around the spacious floor until her flowing black hair took flight with the hem of her swingy cotton dress. "From a real plane ride, not from some cross-country trip on a motorcycle."

"So you're sure that I arrived on two wheels now, eh?" he asked, a wide grin on his square, angular face.

"Of course," Lindy declared faithfully. "Emmy said you never died, so you didn't."

"Of course. So where is Emaline? Not at the Tip Top, I hope."

"No, silly, nothing's open in Hollow Tree Junction on Sundays," she reminded him with an impatient huff. "Emaline drove Mother and Aunt Verna down to Eagle Point to shop. They're awfully busy during the week with the greenhouse to run errands. Of course you showing up and needing a place to stay took up yesterday. Not that anybody minded, though," she hastily added. "Anything for the man that—"

"Don't tell me," he cut in, raising a palm, "who lives in Aunt Verna's bosom."

Lindy wrinkled her nose in mischief. "Who saved Puff-Puff, I was going to say."

"I really didn't do that, you know," he reminded her.

"Gee, I know, Jackie-John." She sighed in disappointment. "But sometimes I forget. Puff-Puff is so real. And you look so different with your hair dyed and your skin, ah, bare." She grinned naughtily. "There's something about your face, too. You look older, wiser. Yes, I believe choosing the law as your life's work was quite right of me, don't you?"

"No."

"Oh, by the way, I have your shirt from yesterday." Lindy skipped to the hallway and returned with his light blue work shirt on a hanger, obviously cleaned and pressed.

"You do that, Lindy?" he exclaimed with pleasure.

"No, dope. Mother did it. Naturally everybody noticed that you didn't bring much along on your Harley. Don't look so invaded," she chided, easily reading his hooded expression. "We all saw your clothes while we were cleaning up the pantry yesterday. What there were of them."

Jackson peeled the shirt off the hanger and slipped it on. It was soft on the skin, despite its sharp creases, sweet and fresh to the nose, as well. Nothing like the cardboard feel left by his laundering jobs. He had to admit the woman's touch was never to be underestimated. Not under this roof, anyway!

"I know what you're thinking," Lindy asserted confidently, rocking on her bare heels. "You're supposed to be a successful lawyer this time around. And how can you pull it off with sparse, worn handyman clothes in your dresser?"

"Not what I was thinking," he said, rolling the sleeves up over his thick forearms. He was pondering his mother-in-law, Margaret. How could her husband have vanished for good, leaving behind his sister, Verna, and dark daughter, Lindy, as bonus reminders? Despite it all, he knew he was destined to return days after he'd flown. The journey had taken several months of searching, wearing at his soul and shoe leather, until he was ultimately satisfied that he was ready to come to terms with Emaline.

Jackson suspected that even blond Emaline must be a reminder to her mother of her bygone husband. A blend of hot Gypsy blood and subtle sensibility behind her dark glittering eyes and fair skin. She could be so hot—as she was in his arms yesterday. She could be so calm—calculating his funeral arrangements.

"Don't worry about the clothes," Lindy announced. "Emmy handled everything."

"Naturally," he agreed magnanimously.

"Told them you were kicking back on vacation because your brother died young and you wanted to taste life on the road while you still had the chance."

"Oh, man, oh, man—that woman!" Jackson clenched his fists at his sides.

"Told them you borrowed the motorcycle for the trip. That you have a real swell car back in Ohio. Four-door tan sedan with air-conditioning."

"She worries way, way too much about details," he muttered ominously.

"Hasn't stopped worryin' since the day you left."

"My funeral should've settled things," he mused grimly. That and all his payments.

"Didn't seem to stop her, though," she insisted with a shrug. "Hungry?"

"As a matter of fact, I am," Jackson realized with a hollow feeling.

"I've been waiting to eat with you." As Lindy went to the cupboard for plates, he opened the refrigerator for a look inside. He grabbed a nearly empty milk carton and opened it, lifting it to his lips.

"Don't drink that!" Lindy squealed, the heavy blue ceramic plates in her shaky hands clanking together.

Jackson pulled the carton away from his mouth, a drop of milk rolling down the corner of his chin.

Lindy set the plates on the kitchen table and rushed up to him. She peered into his gaping mouth as she pulled a tissue out of her skirt pocket to dab the milk from his face. "Looks all clear. You are the biggest fool on earth!" she scolded.

"No harm would come," he protested, shaking the carton for her to see. "I'll finish it all."

"It'll finish you, Jackie-John," Lindy proclaimed dramatically.

"Oh? Oh!" Jackson gulped at the gravity of her words. The carton contained a magical concoction of some sort. "It's not fair to disguise a dangerous substance in a regular carton like that," he complained, wiping his mouth with the back of his hand.

"It's marked," she urged, snatching the carton. "See the cow on the side. See the dot on the cow's forehead?"

"No," he claimed with a stubborn glare.

"Sure, sure." She tapped a pointed red nail on the dot in question. "Looks like the cow has an extra eye, doesn't it?"

"Why all the secrecy? Why not ferment it in a clearly labeled jar?"

"Because snoopy old Colin is always raiding our icebox, and he'd soon catch on," she explained. "It's the cream in his coffee—and tea—these days."

"Verna's work?"

"Yeah. She's just crazy for him."

"I thought your mother..."

"She likes him, too," Lindy said. "They don't admit it out loud, but it's come down to a contest between Mother's natural charms and Aunt Verna's magical ones. Each thinks she alone has the key to Colin's heart. Funny, neither seriously wanted him until the other set her claim."

Jackson sniffed the milk inside the carton.

"Tasteless, odorless," Lindy explained. "But powerful! As anxious as Aunt Verna is to capture Colin, she's limiting him to the smallest doses a day, which isn't hard to control since he's over here all the time."

"Well, thanks for the warning, Gypsy girl." With a shudder Jackson squeezed the carton shut and returned it to the second shelf.

Lindy pushed the fridge door closed, regarding him in wonder. "Lucky I was here. One big gulp of that stuff and we'd have found you out on Route 11 tonight in some pasture mooing at the moon with the real milk makers."

Jackson blanched beneath his tan, dropping into a chair at the table.

"You look odd. Better eat something right away."

"Guess I'm not as hungry as I thought."

"What's the matter? You don't even believe in white magic."

"Just not hungry, that's all," he claimed hoarsely.

"I care about you, you know," she crooned, looping an arm around his neck. "You're the only brother I'll ever have. Having a man around here again is real nice."

Jackson smiled fondly at Lindy, his ally always. "Maybe you'll have an uncle real soon," he teased. "If this milk does the trick."

"I don't know who will win Colin," Lindy griped, annoyed by his teasing. "I don't know if either one of them would really be better off."

"I don't know, either," he agreed.

"He was your friend before," Lindy recalled, her dark eyes shifting with uncertainty.

"Yes, he was. But you can be sure that my first loyalties are under this roof," he assured her, pinching her chin.

"Somebody should find out just what he's up to," Lindy suggested with a look of feigned innocence.

"Somebody like me." He'd inferred her meaning without much trouble.

"Have a man-to-mooch talk with him," Lindy prodded flatly.

Jackson nodded. He knew he was doing it again, getting emotionally involved with all the Holt women. But it was impossible to separate Emaline from the bunch. And in truth he cared for all of them. Despite the fact that they currently cared for him under false colors. That glitch pained him severely. If only they'd approved of the marriage the first time around...maybe he wouldn't have cut out so readily without Emaline. Maybe if he hadn't been so hurt by their ultimate rejection.

But the "what ifs" didn't matter any longer. He was more bewitched by his charming wife than ever. That she believed in a magical wonderland of charms and spells wouldn't deter him from having her forevermore.

Jackson crossed the expanse of lawn separating the Holts' brown saltbox from Colin Sinclair's small green-roofed white clapboard a short time later. Both yards needed a mow—a leaf-mulching mow at that.

Lindy had been correct when she counted Colin among his friends. Jackson made friends wherever he went, but Colin had been memorable, a pal of sorts despite their different backgrounds. Perhaps it was because they were in the same boat. Colin, too, was a little out of place in Hollow Tree Junction. The townsfolk had always pointed to Jackson as the handyman ever so handy with the Holts, with no regular job. Colin was frowned upon as well with his cultured demeanor, British accent and his ability to work out of his home with a computer and a sketch pad. A person had to live in Hollow Tree at least ten years to be accepted. That alone ruled out both men.

Though Jackson liked the Brit, he shared some of Lindy's doubts about him. The author had holed up in his house a lot last summer and fall, claiming to be musing on bigger and better projects. But Jackson was certain he'd heard the unmistakable ping-ping-ping signalling a winner on "The Price is Right" wafting through the side windows on many a weekday, as well as the haunting theme song of a soap opera that Aunt Verna often favored in the afternoon.

Was Colin Sinclair gleaning money from the Holts, playing the gentleman gigolo? He hated to think his dough was supporting some kind of triangular tryst!

Colin didn't answer his front bell. Jackson heard noises from within, however, filtering out of a living room window several feet away. He stomped across the porch and peered inside. To his surprise, the television in the far corner of the sparsely furnished room was dark and silent. Rather, the screen of the computer was alight. And the ping-ping and bursts of applause of last year's game show were replaced by the grind of a printer spouting a paper tail across the worn gold carpet.

"Yo! Colin!" Jackson called several times through the window, eventually summoning Colin from the back of the house. He appeared in a darkened doorway, a thin figure in the shadows.

"Ah, it's you! Come round the back."

Colin was waiting for Jackson in the screened service porch. As he unhooked the green storm door for his guest, Jackson couldn't help but wonder why there was a feeling of secrecy about the place. Colin should be boasting of his latest efforts, showing the town he was productive.

"I've been expecting you," Colin said as he set the timer on his washing machine. With the push of a button, the machine hummed efficiently to life. As so it should, Jackson realized with a skeptical pause. The washer, and the dryer standing beside it, were brand-spankin'-new. Nothing like his old set. Oh, Emaline, he inwardly groaned. Where oh, where has the money gone?

"I hope I'm not disturbing you, Colin." Jackson tried for a jovial tone. "With your muse in action and all."

"Lunchtime, anyway. And as I said, I knew you'd come." Colin moved inside jauntily, beckoning Jackson into the kitchen. Jackson followed, dipping his head at the last minute as he stepped through the low doorframe. He'd forgotten about the low clearance out back. He'd normally called on Colin via his front porch.

"Odd doorway," Colin noted conversationally. "The service porch was built on later, I understand. No doubt by a handyman who didn't know what he was doing." His smiled benignly. "Have a chair while I check on my meal."

Jackson pulled a chair away from the small table and stretched his out long legs. He watched his host turn sizzling circles of bologna in a large black skillet.

"I hope the cooking odor doesn't offend you," Colin called back over his shoulder as he tended to each slice of meat.

"The aroma of prime rib couldn't give me more pleasure at the moment. Lunch meat is a tasty American standby from sea to shining sea."

"A far cry from my potted-meat sandwiches at home, but you're welcome to join me," Colin invited, waving his large fork in the air.

"I'd love to!" Jackson said gratefully.

Colin turned to flash him a wry look, obviously startled by Jackson's unbridled enthusiasm over the budget meal. But he didn't question. He merely got a second plate and utensils and put them on the table. "I have money for some things these days, but I still cut corners when I can." He set about getting bread and iced tea to round off the meal. Once they were seated face-to-face with their sandwiches, Colin spoke again. "So, Jackson, what brings you back to our crop-rich mecca?"

Jackson stared at him, his teeth clamped on his sandwich.

"Well, you are our Jackson Monroe, are you not?" Colin was clearly affronted that he had to prod further. "Dear boy, you are talking to a master of evasion, a finely tuned manipulator. And an old cohort," he added with mild reproof.

"Jackson I am, old friend," he acknowledged, chomping hungrily on his food.

Colin scanned him with merriment. "Well, let me say in only the most beneficent way that Verna's wild red tint doesn't suit you much."

He nodded and swallowed. "Blondes definitely do have more fun. You have any mustard?"

"Help yourself," Colin invited. "What the hell, bring the mayonnaise while you're at it," he added airily once Jackson reached the refrigerator. "I know it's a killer on the cholesterol scale, but this is a celebration of sorts."

Jackson was soon seated again with the goodies, faced with Colin and his questions. "What is the wandering wolf doing back at the henhouse? Does Emaline know just who and what you are?"

"She did this!" he confided the worst, tugging at some tufts of auburn hair, slapping his bare face.

"The clever little minx."

"John doesn't get to smoke, either," he grumbled.

"Nasty habit," Colin affably pointed out.

"Care for a cigar?"

"Splendid, old chap."

Jackson pulled a handful of cigars from his shirt pocket and tossed them on the table. He and Colin lit up, soon puffing with groans of content.

"Do go on, Jackson," Colin invited, his pale blue eyes alight with anticipation, pushing forth a saucer for an ashtray.

"She bumped me off when she thought I wasn't coming back," Jackson said, awe still lingering in his tone.

"Yes, I see." Colin puffed and mused, as if setting the situation straight in his mind. "She rushed off to Norfolk, returned with a kitty..."

"And a box of rocks for me."

"Nothing like closing the lid for good."

"Well, she thought I was gone for good," Jackson theorized.

"Yes, with the father leaving for keeps, I imagine it never occurred to her that you might return," Colin concluded. "They haven't had much luck with keeping men grounded."

"I begged Emaline to come along. But she wouldn't hear of it."

"No, Emaline wouldn't have left her poor, dear family," Colin agreed. "She is totally naïve to many of the more distasteful ways of the world, but she is bright and loyal. She would've viewed taking off as a sign of weakness, betrayal. The sins of the father again, you know."

"The ladies could manage without Emaline," Jackson asserted, draining his iced tea.

Colin nodded in affirmation, refilling Jackson's glass from the plastic pitcher on the table. "Oh, yes, they are clever, to be sure."

"The entire situation is agonizing," Jackson despaired. "I come back here to confess that I've been lying to myself, only to find that Emaline has been lying to everybody else! Now that I've finally smartened up to realize that I can't live without her honest love, genuine compassion, I'm faced with... my brother!"

"It's rather comical, in an ironic sort of way. I venture to say that as John, my boy, you could get away with anything you had a mind to. As the rambler Jackson, you were so limited. Intriguing . . . what a little embellishing can do to one's image."

For the first time all weekend, Jackson felt sated and relaxed. It felt good to talk to another man, to someone who called him by his real name. Their alliance had always been fairly straightforward. Jackson hoped that Colin wasn't up to no good. For now he decided to take him at face value, as the friend he seemed to be. "Can I trouble you for another sandwich?" Jackson asked hesitantly.

Colin's narrow face wrinkled in puzzlement. "Certainly. But with that huge larder next door, I should think—"

"Believe it or not, looks can be deceiving," Jackson corrected dryly, bringing a chuckle to Colin's lips. "Let's just say that for my own peace of mind, I expect to be eating only from the Holt community pots at mealtimes."

"Surely you can be more specific," Colin prompted.

He debated under Colin's scrutiny, then blurted out the news. "Well, Verna's spiking your milk! Maybe other stuff, too!" He hated to betray lovesick auntie, but he had a duty to his fellow man.

"Spiking my milk?" Colin's expression froze, only his pointed nose twitching.

"The milk for your tea and coffee. Some kind of love potion." To Jackson's surprise, Colin's thin mouth curved in amusement.

"I wonder if you could do me a favor, Jackson?"

"What, dump the stuff away?"

"No, not yet. But do find out exactly what Verna is putting in there."

"Are you joking?"

Colin winced in distaste. "You know I'm not much for common jesting. Is this something she concocts from memory?"

"I know she has a book that specifically lists potions. Like a white-magic recipe book," he clarified with a sure nod.

"I must see that book," Colin declared, his dour features animated.

"But why, Colin? Don't tell me you're smitten with Verna?"

Colin closed his eyes momentarily, sighing when he spoke. "I am not at liberty to discuss my intentions yet."

"Honorable intentions?"

"Naturally! Actually, they are both fine women, each in her own unique way," Colin parried. "Margaret is steady, dependable, delicate as one of her own hothouse flowers. Certainly nothing like the kind of woman I'm accustomed to. And there's dear, robust Verna. She's a bit more on the bawdy side with her Gypsy blood, her footloose background. A most interesting woman, as well."

"Then who, as they say on that popular game show, should come on down?"

"We are a delightful threesome as far as I'm concerned. Now, please cooperate with me, Jackson. My cupboards, as meagerly stocked as they are, will be forever open to you."

"It's a deal," he relented out of an equal balance of human decency and a wish to survive. "And I'll throw in a mulch job on your leaves this afternoon."

"Say, that would be very sporting of you," Colin graciously accepted. "By the way, I want you to know I sprang for a tombstone spray in your honor. That is, if you were to meet your demise again, you'd know about my previous effort...." He bowed his head modestly. "It was twenty-nine ninety-five retail."

"Twenty even wholesale from the Holt greenhouse," Jackson smoothly adjusted. "But I'll keep it in mind, if and when I do look down on my next service from the pearly gates. Consider yourself credited with one spray in advance for the real shindig."

Jackson's grin never wavered as he bade farewell. As he crossed the lawns, his mouth curled in a savvy smile. He'd needed that quick reminder at just how easily gentleman Colin could turn a phrase, barter on his own behalf. Imagine, wanting credit for funeral flowers!

Luckily the Brit's intentions would be soon out in the open—he could assure Lindy of that much. He simply had to try to focus on Emaline without allowing outside distractions to overwhelm him.

Jackson raised the Holts' garage door with an easy yank, and proceeded to haul out the old mower. It had obviously been used all spring and summer long, but not taken care of. The blade was caked with dried grass; the engine needed oil.

Jackson stripped off his shirt in the heat of the sun as he set about the task of readying the mower for use. As he worked, he thought about Colin and some of things he'd said during the course of their feast. One remark in particular kept nudging its way to the foreground over and over again.

'As John, my boy, you could get away with anything you had a mind to.'

6

A LAZY, HAZY AUTUMN afternoon in Hollow Tree Junction.

Just like so many other Sundays in the greenhouse, Emaline pondered wistfully. Or could've been so, if not for the sputtering grind of the lawn mower out back. She plunked a third begonia into a hanging pot, banking it with soil. It was impossible to concentrate with that noise! She peered at Jackson as he pushed the old mower across the yard in low-slung cutoffs. His white T-shirt was hanging from the branch of a huge oak near the garage, tossing and billowing in the light warm breeze like a banner proclaiming his masculinity.

Jackson had every reason to be proud of his sturdy, sinewy physique. The broad shoulders, corded limbs and solid stomach had been earned through physical, sometimes strenuous, labor. His morals seemed basically sound, too, despite the more glaring glitch.... Emaline was willing to believe that he was almost the honest man he claimed to be, behaving exactly as he had the first time around—despite the new identity she'd thrust upon him!

Jack was back. Back for her. Untamed, inflexible, but willing to bend over backward for her love. She didn't know she could love anyone so much. Now, if only she could learn to trust him all over again. Resolve the moon curse on the Holts. Tall orders, both.

"Those hanging pots ready for Mrs. Parish, Emaline?" Verna inquired anxiously from the doorway connecting the greenhouse with the mudroom.

"Almost," Emaline replied with a heartfelt sigh.

"They're for Tuesday's harvest celebration, you know." Verna stepped into the glassed structure, beaming over the rows and rows of benches lined with blooming potted plants. "How are you this fine day?" she cooed to a rather large azalea, ablaze with hot-pink petals. "Old Mrs. Witty down Edgecomb Way is going to want you, my lovely darling. And there's my limpy little impatiens!" she gushed. "I'm getting impatient with you...."

Emaline batted not a lash as her aunt weaved her ample form, still encased in the snug jersey print she'd worn shopping that morning, through her plant kingdom. Verna believed that she was running a botanical home for the wayward spirits that dwelt in each and every plant.

"Another example of how plants do indeed use their own body language," Verna lectured. "Take these white impatiens. The stems are far too spindly. They need more light. I told Margaret so last week. She should've paid attention to the body language—"

Verna drew a sharp breath as she was confronted with another form of body language. Jackson's tanned bare back, taut and glistening in the sunshine, left her stammering. "Oh, my. Oh, dear! So strong, so sturdy! So overheated. Poor John should move to the shade," she blustered, drawing a lacy kerchief from the very bosom where Jackson Monroe lived to dab her temples. "Body language is so important to creatures large and small!"

"What are you fussing about, Verna?" Margaret demanded, entering with Lindy on her heels.

"Body John!" Verna exclaimed in wonder. "I mean that John is mowing the lawn."

"Really?" Margaret, looking neat and trim in a cheery red-and-white checked shirtwaist, took a curious peek at the handyman. "Imagine, an attorney who does chores, too. He's so well-rounded."

"A Jack-of-all-trades," Lindy quipped, shoving her hands into the pockets of her orange sunsuit.

Emaline whirled on Lindy with a glower, jabbing the trowel into the bucket of black dirt on the bench. Lindy's dazzling smile dimmed—a watt or so.

"That's not Jackson, Lindy, it's John," Verna corrected, regaining her composure in time to lecture her niece. "Very thoughtless to confuse them—especially when they are so separate."

"He must be trying to overcompensate," Margaret mused kindly. "Trying to fill his blue-collar brother's shoes. You must be more thoughtful, Lindy. Do address him by his true name."

"It was only a joke," Lindy whined.

"Not amusing," Verna said reprovingly.

"You've got it all wrong!" Lindy argued, her face set in discontent.

"You've all missed the point," Emaline erupted suddenly, ripping the gardening gloves from her hands, slamming them on the bench. "You're putting John on a pedestal for cutting the darn grass! Jackson did it all the time! Can't you see that both brothers are well-rounded, and share many of the same wonderful qualities? Jackson's not a lawyer, but he's intelligent, too!"

Margaret and Verna exchanged a look. Emaline was talking about her long-gone husband as if he were out helping his brother trim the hedge. "We think Jackson had many fine traits," Margaret soothed. "Don't we, Verna?"

"There's Puff-Puff," Verna spoke up brightly.

"Before Puff-Puff, before he died," Margaret clarified with a warning look to her sister-in-law.

"I confess to liking John a bit better," Verna trilled stubbornly. "His longer hair, his infectious laugh, his polished manners. It all appeals to me more. I'm sorry."

"But they are so much alike," Emaline insisted. She knew she was treading on dangerous territory, bringing to the surface all of their similarities, but she was caught in her own trap. She hadn't realized how much it would hurt her to know they liked the fictional brother so much more than the real thing.

But he was the real thing! she reminded herself. Jackson was behaving quite true to nature. It was only their perception of him that was different this time around. What a difference a little prejudice—positive or negative—could make!

Verna softened at the sight of her niece's anguished expression and wound a fleshy arm around her, cooing in a tone often reserved for Puff-Puff and her plants. "Don't you fret any longer, Emaline. In retrospect, I do appreciate Jackson's finer points. After all, he was wise enough to choose you as his bride. I assure you, if he were here today right alongside his brother, if he had never gone off to Lincoln and gotten run over, he would receive only the most flattering attention from his aunt Verna."

Lindy rolled her round black eyes, blowing her kinky black bangs sky-high. "You promise, Auntie?" she asked sassily.

"All my statements are promises, young lady," Verna chortled with affront. "You should know that, after sixteen years on this earth! But it is that man out there on whom we must focus now. And he is in need of refreshment," she decided abruptly. "Lemonade! Tangy, sweet lemonade! I'll make it and I'll serve it." With a wave of her kerchief she shimmied past them and toward the house.

"Emaline will serve it," Margaret called after her pleasantly, but firmly.

Emaline nodded mutely. How could she graciously say no after that emotional speech? How could she bear to go near him when he was so very, very hot?

"You've come out of hiding, I see." Jackson's remark was casual as he cast Emaline and her glass of lemonade a brief, sidelong glance. He'd finished the cutting and was in the process of hosing down the mower.

Emaline squeezed the glass tighter, the condensation already forming on its surface, making it slippery beneath her fingertips. She was determined not to lose her grip, on either the drink or her emotions. But he'd barely acknowledged her. An unexpected reaction. Maybe flashy clothing would've caught his attention. She was dressed for work, as he was, a florist smock open over red twill shorts and a scoop-necked black T-shirt. Knowing Jackson, it would've taken a "no clothing" invitation to capture his real interest.

"This old beater hasn't been cleaned since the day Jackson left," he complained, whistling under his breath as though it didn't matter much. Emaline watched as he squatted to tip the old green machine on its side to spray the grimy underside. He aimed the spurting nozzle at the grass-caked blades, the muscles in his thighs and calves corded and flexible, easily balancing him in the awkward position.

"Is that all you can say?" she asked in breathless astonishment.

"It needs a new spark plug, too," he added, tipping his auburn head up to grin at her. The sun caught the highlights in his tinted hair, causing it to dance in rosy-tipped flames. "By the way, thanks for not shaving my chest, or dying it a funny color," he said as she stared down at him. "If you'd botched the job, I would've had to keep my shirt on today."

"A sin against womankind, if my family's reaction is any meter," Emaline complimented tartly.

"Gee whiz, hon, I'm a hit this time around."

"You don't have to be so smug," she chastised, her anger fully exposed.

Jackson bounced to his feet once again, towering over her with a perplexed frown. "What are you so riled up about, anyhow?" He twisted the nozzle to stem the flow of water, gripping it in his clenched first. That hand was the only sign of stress on him. "You created me."

How could she argue the issue? She was hopelessly entangled in her own web of deception! "Well, I wasn't hiding," she eventually spouted petulantly. He was so close now, his low-riding cutoff jeans even a fraction lower on his hard, slippery hipbone. They almost looked as if they could slip off. What a hit he'd be then!

"You've been gone since I got up this morning," he accused. "Don't try to deny that you've been avoiding me."

"We always shop in Eagle Point over the weekend. Mother and Aunt Verna depend on me to take them."

"They can both drive," he interjected quietly.

"I've always taken them," she maintained defensively. Her need to be needed was a raw nerve. "You know there are certain things I do...."

"Some very well," he assented thickly, stroking the hollow of her creamy cheek.

She tossed her thick veil of hair behind her shoulders, stiffening in defense. Even if she could fend him off, how could she defend herself against her internal aches? Knowing that he could fulfill her completely was torment.

"You need a new spark plug, too?" he mocked.

"Stop it," she hissed. "Now."

With a chuckle, he let his finger bypass lips and wander down to her throat. "Don't worry, I'll keep my fingers out of your mouth this time. They're kinda muddy, just like yours. Hey, maybe we should play together," he suggested with boyish delight. "Roll around out here like a couple of pups."

"They're probably watching from the greenhouse," she objected under her breath.

"Watching what?" he challenged.

"Ooo . . ." she fumed, acutely aware of his roughened touch, trailing lower and lower toward the swell of her breast. It had been forever since she'd been touched. It took so little to arouse her. Her husband had been the only one. He would always be the only one.

Emaline squeezed her eyes shut to block the sweet pain of her denial, her lashes moist. She was to meet the same fate as her mother before her. Forever pining for a rambling rogue.

Forever cursed by the light of the moon.

Though Jackson said he would stay this time, he didn't mean it. He couldn't be trusted. She was still waiting for him to confess to past sins. He insisted to want it as before. But there was a debt to deal with first, matters to clear. How could he expect her to believe when he didn't settle up? Some honest man!

But Emaline's heart was beating a tattoo separate from reasonable doubt. Despite his black-hearted behavior, his abandonment, his arrogance, he satisfied her wholly. A telling moan of need escaped her lips.

"Give in," he crooned, calmly fingering a lock of her luxuriant hair.

"You are dirty, sweaty, greasy and uncivilized," she whispered indignantly.

"But ever so handy under both my names. If you turn just a tad to the right," he coaxed silkily, "they can't see what I'm doing."

Emaline whirled sharply out of his reach, lemonade sloshing over the rim of the glass. If only they were alone . . . But one look back confirmed that they were all watching, three anxious heads bobbing behind the glass wall. Lindy actually began to wave! Emaline turned back to Jackson, with a startled gasp. His gaze was delving into her, as if . . . almost as if he were physically penetrating her!

She sizzled at the memories. The hot friction of his flesh driving into her with slicing, poker strokes. So many times she'd cried out his name in the sultry night, coaxing, teasing him on. If he reached out for her now, when she was in this state . . . there would be no controlling either of them.

"Here, you must take this," she offered with abrupt coldness. The verbal anticlimax might have been enough to cool him off, but just to be on the safe side, she deliberately grazed his chest with the icy wet glass. His yelping reply was rude and to the point.

"Sorry," she said meekly.

"I seriously doubt it," he growled under his breath. "But I'll let it all ride for now. This really isn't the time or the place." He paused in helpless wonder. "Somehow you make any time and any place seem right for lovemaking."

Emaline could clearly see he was dry and thirsty. "Take it, John," she urged on a gentler note. "Aunt Verna made it especially for you."

Jackson's hand suddenly snapped back to his side. "What's in it?"

She frowned. "Lemon, water, sugar."

"And maybe just a dash of nettle juice," he accused, recalling one of the family's aphrodisiacs. "Don't give me that innocent look. Lindy told me about Colin's cream!"

"No one is pressuring you into performing."

"That's for sure! But I still don't want any of that stuff," he finished adamantly, thrusting a finger at the glass as if it were filled with venom. "I don't care to lose or gain any attributes."

"Aunt Verna wouldn't dream of diminishing your libido," Emaline scoffed. "Besides, you don't even believe in magic, so why do you care either way?"

"I don't take any chances around here, see? You've done enough hocus-pocus on me for a lifetime."

"I promise there's nothing in here that could possibly harm you," Emaline said to appease him. "And you're so thirsty...."

"Take it away!"

"Afraid something in here might really work?" she jeered. "A big tough guy like you can fend off anything, can't you? Even a wife, for instance?" she added, crimson in anger.

"I'm not the one who needs a love serum." He paused, his expression dangerous. "You drink it, wife. Sip the succulent nectar, loosen up that tight clamshell of yours. Remind yourself of your vow to love, honor and obey. Drink it all up and let's both hope there's something really powerful in there!" With a fiendish look, Jackson turned on the nozzle. When a stream of water spurted forth, he bent his head for a long, sloppy drink.

Emaline's face grew rigid with fury. "I don't need any stimulants, John Monroe!"

"I advise you to stop avoiding me, wife." He lifted his head from the water, a threat etched in the drawn lines of his face.

"I am not hidin' from you," she claimed in a whisper, casting a fervent look back at the greenhouse. "And quit calling me wife around here."

"Just a simple reminder of who you really are," he stated smoothly. "Don't want you to lose sight of the truth."

"And may I say the same to you, mister!"

Jackson froze to scrutinize her in surprise. What the hell was that supposed to mean? "Everything is going to be straightened out, if it's the last thing I do," he vowed forcefully. "For starters, we're going out to dinner."

"Hollow Tree is closed on Sundays," she returned tartly.

"We will go to Eagle Point, to Lincoln, if we have to! But we are going to spend some time alone."

When Emaline opened her mouth for further protest, Jackson wagged a finger at her. "Shall I call on my re-inforcements for help? I'm sure they'd love to see you out on the town with this eligible bachelor."

"You'd use them to manipulate me?" she asked, aghast.

"With pleasure," he fiendishly assured her. "You see, this dog never dreamed he'd have his day in Hollow Tree. I returned fully expecting to be begging forgiveness on bended knee. Thanks to you, I can strut around like the favored son. If you don't like it, end it," he challenged. "Call them out here and expose your charade."

"It's your hide I'm trying to save!" she scolded.

"Dinner at seven, then?" he invited with a knavish smile.

Emaline nodded numbly.

"Fine. Now drink your lemonade love potion like a good girl while I turn off the water at the house."

An angry shot of adrenaline pumped through Emaline as she watched Jackson drop the hose and strut toward the faucet. She had created John for noble purposes, and he was exploiting them all with his gorgeous body and new persona. With a shaky hand, she set the drink on the ground and picked up the hose. She twisted the nozzle to full blast, aiming it at Jackson's spine.

"Agh!" The cold water against his slicked brown skin caused him to contort and roar like a lion. The audience streamed from the greenhouse in protest.

"Shame on you, Emaline," Margaret was the first to admonish.

"I thought it was off," Emaline explained weakly to everyone, her heart hammering wildly in her chest.

Jackson gave the faucet a hard crank, leaving her weapon drippy and useless. He moved back into stalking range, his wild eyes never leaving his quarry.

"I squeezed the biggest lemon for John, and here it sits in the mulch!" Verna remonstrated, tromping through the mushy grass to retrieve the glass.

"John wants me to have it, Aunt Verna." Pent-up emotion escalated to ear-ringing pressure in Emaline's head. She easily cut off her lumbering aunt in one fluid motion, yanking the glass up out of reach. "He claims it'll make me all the more thirsty. Cheers, John!" With that toast she consumed the lemonade in one drippy gulp.

"Emaline!" Hands on hips, Jackson sternly admonished her with a mixture of irritation and awe.

"Stop this instant, Emaline," Aunt Verna admonished.

"This sure beats the bejaggers out of 'One Life to Live,'" Lindy marveled in wonder. "Two lives to live."

"It must be the unseasonal heat today," Margaret noted, groping for a logical explanation. "Forgive her, John, she's been out in the sun too long."

"Wrong plant, Mother Margaret," Jackson muttered to himself. Shame on the moon for drawing him back like a white beacon in the sky. Shame on his moon temptress, who took her energy from the luminescent sphere to bewitch him beyond endurance.

Jackson stood erect in the blazing sun, a bronzed predator studying his shaking, defiant wife. Was she ever hot for him! She practically quaked with lust. So what was holding her back? She needn't fear he'd pounce on her now in the yard. She had to come halfway. And soon she would. The moon would soon be in full bloom in two days' time, making night into day, making her wanton. She'd been damn near insatiable at last year's harvest.... Soon, he'd plant his seed; soon, he'd reap his rewards.

"YOU REMEMBERED THE WINE."

"Chablis isn't that hard to remember, Emaline."

Emaline's expression was strained behind the flickering candle on the table between them. "Are you making fun of me because I don't know much about wine? Because you think I'm a small-town innocent?"

"You are a small-town innocent," he declared, slicing another piece off his juicy steak, popping it into his mouth. He'd missed Eagle Point's Lantren Grill nearly as much as his wife. They made the best steak and cottage fries in the country. Realizing she was fuming over his careless remark, he reached across the beige tablecloth to squeeze her fingers. "It is not my intention to row with you, Emaline. Though after that cold blast of water this afternoon—" he paused to reconsider "—I'd be well within my rights to retaliate."

They really hadn't talked since that confrontation. They were never alone in the rambling house again. Verbal communication had been impossible on the twenty-mile motorcycle ride, as well.

"I just felt you needed cooling off," she replied.

"I've been exhibiting iceburg control without any help from a hose. It was very, very naughty."

"Look, Jackson, I don't want to talk about this afternoon," she declared with an injured look.

"You have a way of evading anything inconvenient," he complained, squeezing her hand harder. "Like a by-gone husband, for instance."

Emaline's exotic eyes flinted with panic over his bitter remark. "If you've taken me here to be mean, I want to go home."

"Dear woman, I've traveled hundreds of miles to see you," he reminded resolutely. And what a sight she was, with her hair swept up in rhinestone combs, her cheeks as flushed as her rose-colored sweater. "What I wanted to say to you since the start—" he faltered "—what I haven't calmed down enough to say, is that I've seen the error of my ways, wife. I'm sorry that I left. I'd never settled long in any one place. And with the entire town against us, leaving seemed to be the practical solution. To tell you the truth, I never thought you'd call my bluff and stay behind."

"So you just roared off."

Jackson released her hand, reaching for his wineglass. "I am a lifelong rambler, Emaline. You knew that when you coaxed me into marriage."

"You wanted to marry me, Jackson Monroe!"

"I wanted to bed you," he pronounced flatly. His eyes glinted over the candlelight, and his tone dropped to a velvety caress as he made a proposal of another kind. "If you let me back into our bed tonight, I'll answer to any name you say. Ralph, George, Puddin' Head."

"This isn't funny," she gasped in affront.

"I have to laugh, wife. I have to laugh or I'll punch a hole in something. And what good is a handyman with a bum hand?" He paused, his mouth taking a cynical curl. "Oh, well, there always is my second calling . . . the law."

"First you say I forced you into marriage. Then you say you want to be my husband." She shook her honey-blond tresses. "I don't understand you."

"Understand that I have my faults. Accept that I'm back to set things right."

"The pain of your rejection sliced my heart in two," she confessed.

"I'd like to say I should've known better, but I did not," Jackson explained. "My father being a handyman, my mother dead, there was no taste of a home and hearth in my background. Moving along was the natural course of life for me. All I ever knew. My basic education was out of library books and a fleeting succession of schools—whenever we stayed anywhere for more than a week's time. Most of my learning came from my father. I was Dad's apprentice in every way. I was at his side as he painted, hammered, fiddled with the plumbing in small towns from here to the California coast."

"Taught you about the ladies, too," she added tartly.

"Not really. When Pa made a conquest, I was shuffled off to the local library," he confided with a twinkle. "You'd be surprised just how many ladies were interested in him. Physical pleasure without commitment isn't exactly a discovery of our generation, you know. Read a shelf load of books on the Civil War one cold November week in Waterloo, Iowa." A reminiscent smile lit his face with boyish delight. "Dad was a good-lookin' fellow. An honest man. But he didn't teach me the value of staying put to make a relationship work. Guess I haven't managed to hang on to anything of value over the years. As a kid I had my feather pillow... but that ended up ashes in a motel fire twelve years ago. The same fire that took Andy Monroe's life, unfortunately. The bittersweet truth is," he confided contritely, "I had to leave to find my way back to you for keeps."

"I'm feelin' sorry for you and you don't deserve it," Emaline murmured. "You never told me about your father before, either."

"We never talked much about anything."

"Sure we did," Emaline protested, gulping her wine.

"About surface things," he claimed, refilling her glass from the carafe. "With your father stamped a deserter, I couldn't imagine you understanding about my pa. I didn't want you to condemn him, lump him in a category with yours. Guess the apple doesn't fall far from the tree sometimes, does it?" he mused apologetically.

"Maybe not on our tree, either. There's been times I've wished I'd gone along with you," Emaline confessed, smiling over the flickering flame.

"Really?"

"But most of the time I hated you and yearned for you at the same time," she told him dourly. "But you've come back. That's what matters most to me now."

"Are you sure you love me?" he asked ruefully.

"Of course I'm sure I do!"

He leaned over his plate. "Then what's the damn problem with our lovemaking? I've always been true and I'll never leave you again."

"Our fate is out of our hands," she insisted mournfully, nibbling on a cottage fry. "It's up to the moon, Jackson. We couldn't control it then, we can't control it now."

"The moon is good luck for us," he argued.

"I thought it was, too," she whispered. "We should never have made love on the night of the harvest moon. It destroyed our marriage."

He stared at her in unblinking incredulity. "I just gave you the explanation as to why I left—why I returned."

She leaned forward, her clammy hand squeezing his. "It happened to my parents in exactly the same way. The moon, the cornfield, the celebration, the…the sex," she finished in a self-conscious hush.

"I can't believe your mother feels—"

"Aunt Verna told Lindy and me," Emaline explained.

"Figures!" he snorted in contempt, staring off into the cedar-paneled room, as if searching for a secret cache of patience.

"She is an expert on white magic," Emaline insisted. "Mind you, I knew it was in the family as we lay on the moist earth that night a year ago. But I didn't think those things passed on to future generations! Perhaps if we'd meditated on the moonstone during the month preceding the harvest moon," she mused, fingering the pearly pendant at her throat. "It would've been enough to counteract the curse."

"The blazes. Damnation and the blazes!" he growled, causing some nearby grill patrons to regard them in sur-

NO RISK, NO OBLIGATION TO BUY...NOW OR EVER!

GUARANTEED

PLAY "ROLL A DOUBLE" AND GET AS MANY AS FIVE GIFTS!

HERE'S HOW TO PLAY:

1. Peel off label from front cover. Place it in space provided at right. With a coin, carefully scratch off the silver dice. This makes you eligible to receive two or more free books, and possibly another gift, depending on what is revealed beneath the scratch-off area.

2. You'll receive brand-new Harlequin Temptation® novels. When you return this card, we'll rush you the books and gift you qualify for ABSOLUTELY FREE!

3. Then, if we don't hear from you, every month, we'll send you 4 additional novels to read and enjoy. You can return them and owe nothing, but if you decide to keep them, you'll pay only $2.69 per book—a saving of 30¢ each off the cover price.

4. When you subscribe to the Harlequin Reader Service®, you'll also get our newsletter, as well as additional free gifts from time to time.

5. You must be completely satisfied. You may cancel at any time simply by sending us a note or a shipping statement marked ''cancel'' or by returning any shipment to us at our expense.

The Austrian crystal sparkles like a diamond! And it's carefully set in a romantic "Key to Your Heart" pendant on a generous 18" chain. The entire necklace is yours free as added thanks for giving our Reader Service a try!

DETACH AND MAIL CARD TODAY!

HARLEQUIN "NO RISK" GUARANTEE

- You're not required to buy a single book—ever!
- You must be completely satisfied or you may cancel at any time simply by sending us a note or shipping statement marked "cancel" or by returning any shipment to us at our cost. Either way, you will receive no more books; you'll have no obligation to buy.
- The free books and gift you claimed on this "Roll A Double" offer remain yours to keep no matter what you decide.

If offer card is missing, please write to: Harlequin Reader Service, 3010 Walden Ave., P.O. Box 1867, Buffalo, NY 14269-1867 prise. She was holding out on him because of some superstition.

"I can only tell you I love you. That I will never let you out of my sight again!" His tone lowered, and his features softened. "I feel so lost in that two-bit town of yours, in our marriage. Why can't we tell folks who I really am? The humiliation won't last for long. And why are you working for Milt Dooley? I've been sending you money."

He could certainly figure out that it was all woven together if he wanted to! It was her final test to his loyalty. If he failed, there was no point at all in telling folks that Jackson Monroe still lived. Her defenses rose, hardening her tone. "I have to do my part. Fulfill family obligations."

"Is that all you can tell me?" he asked, aghast at her tight-lipped expression.

"I can tell you that I'm going to search like mad for a cure to our curse in the old family books. Don't you have anything else you'd like to tell me?"

Jackson drew a dubious frown. "Not that I can think of . . ."

If only he'd own up to what he'd done without force! Emaline closed her eyes, summoning all the shreds of patience she had left. She would not accuse him of anything. If he was truly the contrite, honest man he claimed, he would make it all right. "I am willing to wait," she told him nobly, a forced smile tipping her lips.

"Somehow I'm going to straighten all of this out." Rising he pulled out her chair. "Shall we go?"

He was in love with a crazy person! Jackson could feel Emaline's arms tighten around his middle as he took a couple of turns along the dark country roads a bit too sharply. Realizing his carelessness, he eased back on the gas. He didn't wish to frighten her or put her in peril. No, what he wanted to do was ease the bike into the ditch and pull her into the open field flanking the road. He wanted to make sweet love to her until she cried in abandon. One roll in the hay—or corn—would put him in control once again.

How could she really believe their love was doomed? There was no mystical connection between him and his father-in-law and the moon! Willie Holt was a Gypsy who worked the carney circuit, who preferred to wander. Logic and simple deduction explained away everything.

Emaline buried her head in Jackson's solid back as they whizzed into the night. The moon was ripe above them in the velvet sky, teasing, beckoning. He had to be tempted to stop the bike and take her atop the cool ground. She tensed with every jolt, every curve.

In the end, Jackson did nothing. He drove directly home, carefully parking the cycle in the garage beside the family sedan. He offered her a chaste hand in the privacy of the garage. Together they rounded the house where Margaret and Verna where sitting peacefully on the porch swing.

"Back so soon?" Verna greeted them, turning off the radio nestled between them.

"Yes," Emaline replied with a breath of relief, allowing Jackson to lead her up the brown wooden steps. It was over! He hadn't tempted her with as much as a caress.

"How was the dinner?" Margaret asked, setting aside her knitting.

"The pounded steak special was wonderful," Jackson told them.

"Wonderful," Emaline concurred dreamily, resting her head on his sturdy forearm. She'd never felt closer to her husband than she did at that moment. The confidences they'd shared had strengthened their bond. Jackson had never been so forthright before. And he claimed he wanted to make things right. She'd work on the curse. It would be fine.

"I knew he'd like that steak," Verna was prattling on, "It was one of Jackson's favorites."

Jackson planted a kiss on the top of Emaline's head. "Shall I tell them, sweet, or would you like the honor?"

Emaline raised her head and regarded his rakish look in bemusement. She'd missed a spot in the conversation. No doubt because she was a big groggy from the two glasses of wine and the rocky ride home. "You, ah, could tell them, I s'pose . . ." she invited in a faraway voice.

"Very well," he cut in swiftly, hooking his arm around her waist to bear the limpness no doubt to follow. "Hold on to your swing chains now, ladies," he proclaimed. "Emaline and I are engaged!"

7

"ENGAGED TO BE MARRIED?" Margaret's knitting slipped out of her lap as she sprang up with unbridled enthusiasm.

"The very same," Jackson affirmed proudly.

Squeals of disbelief rang through the night air, Emaline's the squeakiest.

"I know it must seem sudden to you ladies," he intoned, his arm vise-like on her squirmy spine. "But Emaline and I cannot deny our mutual attraction. Whatever sparks flew between her and my brother have caught us by surprise, engulfed us in flames."

Emaline watched in horror as her elders sprang forth, pushing her aside to kiss and nuzzle their new addition-to-be. They loved the idea of this marriage. To a man they thought they'd known for two short days!

"Our Emaline finally snagged herself another man!" Verna bubbled to Margaret, clasping her hands together in glee.

"And a lawyer," Margaret responded in turn, as if they were alone.

No one but Emaline noticed that John the groom had to bite his lip over that one, ultimately managing to retain his jolly grin. The conniving lout!

"Oh, this is serendipity," Verna said giddily. "First John, next Colin."

"What about Colin?" Margaret, who was in the process of stuffing her knitting materials in her fabric sack, paused.

Verna, setting a hand on her cushiony hip said, "Well, no matter who wins his heart, there will be a second marriage in the wings."

"Not in front of the children," Margaret admonished.

"Surely they know of our little rivalry," Verna huffed impatiently. "The powers of the universe pitted against your blueberry muffins and Swiss steak."

"Let's continue this discussion inside," Margaret proposed, yanking open the screen door.

The moment the bickering women were inside the house, Emaline whirled on her intended. "I should've known you couldn't be trusted!"

"I can't be trusted?" he asked, running a hand over his shaven face.

"I thought we reached a new understanding tonight. How dare you play a trick like this?"

"A man only lives seventy-odd years total. Take away one's boyhood, and that leaves precious little sack time."

"We're already married," she needlessly reminded him. "What on earth do you hope to gain by this little trick?"

"It gives me permission to touch you anytime I want," he returned smugly. "Smooch the daylights out of you with their blessing." She raised a threatening fist, which he snagged with a chuckle. "Allow me to demonstrate."

Emaline's lungs emptied as he thrust her against his length. He swiftly smothered her sounds of protest with lips. His tongue forged into her mouth like liquid fire, jolting her whole system into shivering sensitivity. Her protests ebbed away as his hands roamed her back, her hips, molding her to him like a languid doll. She clung to him hungrily, sapping his favors, offering her own.

It was the seducer Jackson who ultimately broke free with a heaving breath. Though not one button or zipper had been loosened, he was on the verge of no return. "Be wild, be wicked, take your new fiancé to your room tonight," he puffed unsteadily, running a shaky hand through her mussed hair. When Emaline cast a foreboding look at the glowing moon, he lowered the hand to her eyes. "We'll just pull the shades and forget everything else," he prodded.

"Your ability to forget is darn amazing," she fumed, tearing his hand from her face. His look of stark betrayal softened her disposition. "But believe me, sweet baby, I'm going to do everything in my power to find a cure for the curse. I just need time."

"You've got till the harvest moon celebration," he said with frustrated reluctance. "You see, wife, I still believe the moon is lucky for us. It's about the only superstitious belief I have." He took a couple of steps across the porch, pivoting to thrust a finger at her. "That . . . that night we spent loving each other last year. That was the greatest night of my life," he confessed with raw emotion. "So nobody, nobody is going to convince me there is a moonstruck curse upon us."

"What if I fail in my quest, sweet baby?" she whispered, her dark eyes somber.

"Then I will love you, anyway, and prove our good luck!" he proclaimed savagely.

"But it would again mean ruin for us!"

"Then for your own sake, I suggest you start reading up on this curse of yours tonight!" He stomped off the steps and crossed the lawn with giant strides, leaving her alone with her fears.

EMALINE WAS CARESSING his feet.

With a groggy groan of ecstasy, Jackson stretched and

turned on the creaky rollaway bed, the discomfort of the squishy mattress fading into the background of his mind.

Reality and fantasy were again merging, teasing at the edges of his consciousness. But the rub was real—he was sure of it. The pressure on his toes, the tickle on his arch...it followed him even as he instinctively drew away. She wasn't being her subtle self, though. The feathery touch was almost torturous.

"You are such a naughty one," a rich voice tittered through the cloudy caverns of his mind, snapping him to attention like the sharp snap of a leash.

Emaline did not titter. Ever.

Jackson's body stiffened on the mattress, his moans of pleasure silenced between locked lips. If not Emaline, who...

It just couldn't be. Could it? With heart thumping, he forced his crinkled eyes open. Dear lord in heaven, it was true. There was no mistaking the bobbing auburn head of his kindred spirit at the foot of the bed. Aunt Verna had stripped back his covers and was rummaging through them!

Jackson suddenly realized he was nearly naked before her again, and this time it was more skin than his chin. He was clad only in his underwear. She was dressed in one of her flowing fortune-teller dresses, up to something magical, no doubt. The bosom where he lived was quaking in its foundation as she bent forward jerkily, mumbling something under her breath. An incantation? For what?

"Oh, my, John!" Verna's head snapped up as a growl erupted from his throat. "Among the living, I see."

"I've always considered myself a member of that happy bunch." Jackson stared down at the fluffy patchwork quilt and blue blanket torn loose and piled out of reach at the opposite end of the bed. The closest linen was his sheet, heaped at his knees. A tightness gripped his throat.

"Wouldn't you just know it, dear?" she paused her pawing to ask.

His heart jackhammered. "Know what?"

"Kismet, dear heart," she purred.

"Kis-a-met?" he repeated hoarsely. One sharp yank brought the sheet up out of the pile to his chin.

"Stop your teasing," she chortled, clapping her bejeweled hands together sharply.

"Emaline know about this?"

"No sense troubling Emaline," Verna poo-poohed.

A tantalizing wisp brushed against his feet suddenly, causing Jackson to yelp. How'd she do that with both hands in the air?

"You, John Monroe, are a conspirator," she chided in a triumphant singsong.

A wave of claustrophobia engulfed him. Jackson edged back, back, on the mattress until he was propped up to the white-paneled wall. The cramped pantry began to shrink to even smaller proportions under her beady gaze. Cornered, he took the offensive, arching his heavy brows, leveling a gunmetal-gray glare at her.

"You and she are coconspirators," Verna continued to scold.

He and Emaline? What did she really know? Aunt Verna loved games. Almost as much as her hothouse plants.

"Come to me, precious, and let me rub your hairy tummy!" With that frightening proclamation, she peeled back the quilt and blanket with a sweeping magician's flourish, causing them to fall over his head in a scented heap.

Jackson fumbled under the bedding, not releasing a breath until he found the light of day again. To his amazement, Verna was just scooping Puff-Puff off the foot of the mattress. She'd been talking to the cat! It was her hairy tummy Verna was speaking of!

"You see now, John," she said, holding the white, mewing creature up to her cheek. "Pure kismet that she crept into bed with you. She knows who you are."

"Who might that be?" he demanded warily.

"The brother of the man who saved her life!"

"Oh, yeah," he mumbled, rubbing the stubble pricking through his skin.

"That bit of whisker makes you even more dashing," she ventured, hovering closer.

Jackson's beard had been considered wild, he recalled with a bitter twinge. He cleared his throat, struggling to keep his voice level. "Didn't my brother also wear some hair on his face? Many thought he was quite debonair."

Verna tsked with forced patience. "Forgive me, John, but you just have an aura about you that can't be denied. Jackson, though certainly brave, didn't wear his whiskers the way you do, dear."

"I see." Only too well! How stubborn, hypocritical Auntie would fume when she discovered John was a figment of Emaline's imagination.

"Animals have a keen sense of people," Verna continued with authority. "They—"

"Mornin'." Lindy sidled into the room, her hips swaying beneath the ribbed bottom of a long rosy pink sweater, her long legs encased in purple tights. "What are you two doing?" she demanded with the exuberance of one joining a party game.

"Caught him red-handed!" Verna announced with a tinkle of laughter.

Lindy's eyes traveled from Jackson's bare, hair-dusted legs in the tossed bed to the faded, belted jeans hanging over a rickety wicker chair. "In hot water again?"

"Do you ladies mind?" he thundered, his patience snapping as cleanly as a dry autumn twig.

"No need to get so huffy, boomerang boy," Lindy snipped, extending a pouting lip which nearly could've accommodated the white china cup and sauce in her hands. "Here's the tea, Auntie."

"Give it to John, *posh*," she directed in businesslike briskness.

Jackson knew he was in for another fortune. And maybe more, depending on the contents of the tea itself.

"Auntie wants to read your leaves," Lindy verified coyly as he accepted the cup. "She figures something went kerflooie the last time."

"A short circuit in the power?" he commented lightly.

"I have a reputation to maintain here in town for my accurate dukkerin'," Verna countered seriously, setting down Puff-Puff.

Jackson remembered that fortune-telling often preceded transactions out in the greenhouse by Verna, or one of the nieces if she wasn't available.

"Drink up," Verna prompted as he frowned at the liquid in hesitation. "Unless you want lemon, or sugar or milk."

"No milk!" he barked, slicing the air with his hand. "No—no, nothing!"

"It's just plain old tea," Lindy assured him sincerely, suppressing a smile.

"Okay." Jackson took small hasty sips, conceding that it did taste wonderful. He then flipped over the cup and turned it just as he had so many times before.

"Good boy." Verna took the cup and righted it for examination.

"Could you take it to the kitchen?" Jackson requested.

"Can't risk unsettling the leaf patterns," Verna clipped in response, engrossed in her reading. "A wig?" she blustered, her eyes narrowing in distrust. "Deception, falsehoods . . . It can't be."

"Maybe it's a duck," Lindy hastened to add as a diversion, peering over Verna's fleshy arm. "Good news, the duck."

"Silly *poshrat*." She looked over at Jackson. "I see a cat, too. Secret enemies, John. Swindles in business. Any pending cases back in Ohio?"

"My calendar is clear," Jackson adamantly insisted, folding his arms across his bare chest.

"Maybe the cast crossed signals with Puff-Puff," everhelpful Lindy suggested, favoring Jackson with a bolstering nod and a wink.

"Perhaps the leaves are a faulty crop," Jackson suggested.

"Perhaps," Verna conceded thoughtfully. "Emaline had an ear in her cup this very morn. Why should my innocent fair-haired *posh* beware of scandal?" She paused to inhale a homily-size breath. Jackson hurried to cut her off.

"I would like a little privacy now," he announced with as much dignity as he could muster in his vulnerable state of dress.

"Another cup of tea—" Verna hastened to offer. "The pot is steeping."

"I am steeping, Aunt Verna," Jackson announced tightly. "I don't expect a house of women to be familiar with the male code. But it's every man's right to put his pants on alone."

"But, my boy—"

"The tea party is over!"

"Very well," Verna relented in compromise. "I suppose a man's private quarters is no place for an innocent like Lindy." With a toss of her auburn-sunset pin curls, Verna exited with her reluctant niece in tow.

Where was Emaline when he needed her? Jackson wasted no time hopping out of bed to yank on fresh jeans and pull a white T-shirt over his reddish-brown head. Cursory inspection in his dresser-top mirror confirmed that his hair tint was fading just a fraction, revealing the faintest golden hue. Combine this development with the morning stubble on his face, and there was a much welcome emergence of the true man inside. This honest glimpse gave him buoyancy.

Jackson soon moved into the airy yellow kitchen stocked with ancient appliances and shelves of bric-a-brac. Amazingly, Verna and Lindy were nowhere in sight. Margaret, the family anchor, was seated alone at the scarred pine table, poring over some bills and ledgers. He took in her conservative gray dress with the pleated skirt and buttoned Peter Pan collar. Her blond hair was pulled up in a braided coronet, her face colored only with a streak of dark pink lipstick. Though his mother-in-law's reserved nature had been a negative force in his marriage to Emaline, it always had given the house a calming, realistic balance. And bless her conservative heart, she wouldn't be caught dead or otherwise digging around under a man's covers.

"Hello, John," she greeted him, her green eyes clouded as she set her pencil down on the stack of papers.

"Good morning, Margaret," he replied cheerily.

"You're just the man I need," she confessed, a girlish smile hovering on her forthright face. "I sent the others away so we could be alone."

She, too? Jackson's knees began to quake, so he took a chair beside her. Perhaps it had been better the first time around. Emaline had been the only one who needed him, paid much attention to him. He'd never realized just how busy a fox could be in a houseful of anxious hens. John Monroe was clearly too much of a good thing!

"It seems a man is just what we need around here," she ventured tentatively. "It was so nice the way you mulched the lawn yesterday. . . ."

"I'm fairly handy with tools," he admitted with pride. "If you have a leaky faucet, or a loose floorboard, I—"

"Oh, my, no." Margaret gave his arm a halting pat. "Don't get me wrong—I'm sure you can work with your hands well enough, but it's your specialty that I need today."

"Specialty?" he tested the word with apprehension.

"I have some legalities to straighten out concerning our florist business."

"You have some legal questions?" he hastened to clarify, struggling to suppress his shock. First Verna's kitty, now this! The blows just kept coming.

"Shall I tell you now? Or if you wish, Verna could fix you something to eat first."

If that was a veiled threat, it was a persuasive one! "Go ahead," he encouraged hastily. "Don't call Verna back on my account."

"Well, a local woman named Loretta Gilbert tripped over our back greenhouse stoop a few weeks ago," Margaret began rather awkwardly, toying with her pencil. "Unfortunately, she reached out for a rickety trellis I had instructed Verna to take down. I admit it was a hazard.... Anyway, as back luck would have it, Loretta took the trellis down for us, in a very upsetting tumble onto the lawn. Naturally it wasn't funny," she assured him to cancel the smile twitching at the corner of her mouth. "Though she did make quite a scene out of it.

"We got her into the house and Verna massaged her neck with some herbal salve that is supposed to cure everything but the mange. Loretta claimed to be nothing more than flustered at the time. Now she's telling the members of her sewing circle that the crick in her neck is far worse than usual because of her accident over here. She's threatening to sue us!"

Jackson rubbed his face in contemplation. His very first lawsuit. And he'd only been in the profession a few days. Took him longer to find the simplest handiwork the last time he blew into town. Maybe there was something to this attorney gig! Naw, he decided, looking into Margaret's open face. But wouldn't it serve Emaline right if he took on the case!

"What do you think?" Margaret eventually asked, biting her lip.

"If you really want my opinion," Jackson began awkwardly under her trusting gaze. "I would pay her a visit, discuss her position. Maybe this sewing club of hers is just a catchall for everyone's gripes."

"I shall approach her at the harvest picnic," Margaret decided, brightening.

"If the going gets tough, you can always fall back on legal action," Jackson pointed out, patting her hand. "Me, I prefer to take the easy, honest way out whenever possible."

"What a lovely sentiment," Margaret marveled. "Many attorneys are anxious to get to court."

"I rely heavily on plain old common sense," he informed her, pushing back his chair from the table. "Now, maybe you can tell me where Emaline is this morning."

"Why, at work, of course," Margaret replied casually, her eyes back on her paperwork.

"At the Tip Top? I thought she worked a later shift!"

His harsh tone drew her full attention. "Only on Fridays. Does it matter, John?"

Matter? He'd planned to confront her in front of the others, insist that the wife of Jackson Monroe didn't have to work. The underhand trick had worked so well last night with the engagement. "She doesn't need to work anymore, Margaret," he explained to his audience of one. "We'll soon be married and I can easily support us both."

Margaret beamed approvingly. "I am so glad to hear it, John. To be perfectly candid, I never did care for her working at the café. I grew up with Milton Dooley here in Hollow Tree, and he was rather unsavory, even as a boy. Stole things from the grocer, vandalized teachers' cars—nasty things like that. He always seemed to walk the fine line between crime and prank."

"So, why, Margaret, why?" he demanded in disgust.

"Why does Emaline put up with him?" Margaret sifted through her papers and extracted a large business checkbook. Jackson stood over her shoulder as her rounded unpolished fingernail skimmed the figures entered in the list of accounts. "Just look at the generous salary he gives her, John." She tapped the book at particular monthly installments. "Cash every month."

Jackson clenched his fists at his side, drawing air in between his gritted teeth. The figures entered in Margaret's distinct hand were all the same amount, a quite familiar amount. He'd found the missing money! For some strange reason, Emaline was depositing his crisp hundred-dollar bills into the family accounts, claiming they were paychecks from the Tip Top Café! But why? What would she gain by doing that? Why not just say the late Jackson had a life insurance policy? Emaline had plenty to do right here with the household and greenhouse. Why go out looking for another job? Especially with the town slimeball? Furthermore, where was the salary from the Tip Top? He prayed that lothario Colin wasn't taking it. Wherever her salary was going, that creep Dooley wasn't paying Emaline anything near the figure under Margaret's fingernail. How could Lindy and the ladies be so naïve as to believe such nonsense?

Jackson shook his auburn head in wonder at his own bemusement. What a rhetorical question! They believed everything and anything Emaline told them! He was living proof of it!

"Are you all right, John?" Margaret asked solicitously, rising to press a hand to his forehead. "You are so drawn. You need nourishment."

"I have to see about Emaline," he declined, distancing himself mentally and physically.

"Maybe you could shake some sense into her," Margaret encouraged, dropping back into her chair. "Heaven knows I've tried, despite the fact that the money's been handy."

"It'll all be over very soon, Margaret, I promise you."

"Wonderful. I can't tell you how happy I am that you and Emaline are going to be married," she confided. "She's so delicate."

Hah! Emaline was no weakling. But she did need direction. For starters, a firm hand steering her out of the Tip Top Café.

"Psst!"

Jackson was wheeling his Harley out of the garage a short time later when he spotted Colin motioning to him from his service porch across the lawns. Jackson waved, but continued pushing the cycle. He was dressed in his tan twill pants and a royal blue shirt, so it should have been obvious to the Brit that he had plans. Did he ever have plans! Laying out a formidable course of action had soothed his sharpened nerves, eased the knot of frustration in his gut. It was no time for a neighborly call.

"Come over here!" Colin called from his back stoop, his long, thin arm windmilling at Jackson.

Jackson shook his head emphatically. "No time."

"Give you breakfast," Colin coaxed.

"Sorry." Jackson eased onto the smooth black leather seat of the bike, kicking up the stand with the heel of his boot.

Colin dashed across the grass like a maroon-clothed pelican as Jackson adjusted his rearview mirror. "Have you had a chance to ferret out the potion book?"

Jackson pulled his steel-rimmed sunglasses out of the his pocket and adjusted them, all the while regarding the other man. Colin Sinclair was a roguish sort, despite his frayed oxford shirts in various patterns and baggy corduroy pants in assorted colors and wales. There was always an unmistakable cynicism in his British inflection and a blue topaz glitter to his pale eyes that belied any helpless claims. "I haven't had the chance to investigate yet," Jackson apologized genially.

"But you promised me you would," Colin upbraided him, his aristocratic features sulky.

Jackson patted the older man's slight shoulder with a heavy hand of consolation. "I'll come through just as I promised. All of those potions make me jumpy, too. Still, I don't understand why you want the recipes."

"You'll find out soon enough," Colin said evasively, openly appeased by Jackson's guarantee. "I know I may seem abrupt on this issue, old chum, but I am desperate, with little time left."

"No man can top my desperation at the moment," Jackson muttered.

"Hmm, yes," Colin conceded with a nod. "One does tend to get wound up in one's own difficulties. Any new developments at the henhouse?"

"Margaret has some legal difficulties for John to untangle."

"Loretta's crick in the neck?"

"Yeah. I gave her some good, sensible advice."

"The handyman special?" Colin quipped with a lift to his gray brow. A brow that fell fast under Jackson's unamused glare. "Sorry about that. If she does eventually need a more experienced litigator, Walter Grimm is a competent man. Has his own practice in Eagle Point on Fifth Avenue."

"What I need today is the name of a good jeweler. I'm buying a diamond ring."

"Cross Brothers on the same street is reputable. Care to explain?"

"I'm engaged," Jackson happily informed him.

"Really now," Colin extended a hand in jolly good will. "To your wife, I presume."

"The very same," Jackson affirmed as they shook hands.

"Must've been quite a surprise to the household, after only a couple of days in town."

"Emaline was the most astonished, I think," he said with a broad grin of satisfaction. "I sort of announced it to all of them at the same time, you see. When the ladies chirped with approval, there was little Emaline could say."

Colin shook a chiding finger at him. "I believe you're growing as wily as the rest of us."

"Just trying to beat the system."

"Sporting of you to pop for another bauble," the ever-economical Colin observed.

"Emaline didn't have a diamond the first time around, only her gold band. I plan to do it up right this time."

"Ah."

"Well, it's off to Eagle Point, then the Tip Top."

"Even my cornflakes are better than Eggs Benedict Arnold at Dooley's place," Colin sniffed with affront.

"Not going for the cuisine."

"Oh?"

"Going to get Emaline fired." When Colin frowned in surprise, he added tersely. "No wife of mine is working in that dive."

"But why would you go about getting her discharged?" Colin asked in bewilderment. "Just tell her to quit."

"I did. She won't."

"Curious . . ."

From behind the shelter of his dark lenses, Jackson watched Colin ponder the puzzle. Was the dry-tongued English gent what he appeared to be, or was he a cad putting the squeeze on Emaline?

"Perhaps she's holding tight to her independence," Colin said thoughtfully, seemingly oblivious to Jackson's inner struggle. "Maybe she needs time away from the mother hens. I've often wondered why Dooley, though. Maybe it's repressed spite. She knows you and Dooley squared off over that carpentry work you did in his café. Perhaps she felt it was the ultimate slam to her runaway husband."

Jackson put his helmet on his head, a sour taste on his tongue as the possibility sank in. "I'll get to the bottom of it," he vowed with a twinge of forewarning, just enough to unbalance a guilty rogue. He wanted to be fair, so assumptions simply were not enough. He needed proof before he would act.

"The best of luck," Colin offered breezily, not appearing a bit intimidated. He turned on his heel and was off with a jaunty step as Jackson coasted down the length of the driveway.

Jackson roared off down the tree-lined street, blowing off steam with an extra squeeze on the accelerator beneath his hands. He was always in control while on his cycle, whether he was in Miami or Maine. Everything was real. The color and texture of the countryside, the wind on his face. He was coiled nearly to the snapping point over this entire fiasco. He was being denied his basic rights.

Sex. Truth. Sex!

Actually, the truth was as important to him as the sex. His quest to instill both in his marriage was burning internally with forest fire voracity. Unfortunately nothing in Hollow Tree seemed real to him, with its picturebook landscape, its quirky citizens. For a man who lived on his wits, who had faced harsh reality since childhood, he found it difficult to believe that Hollow Tree Junction still existed in modern times. Why, Emaline's charade concerning him could be the biggest crime to hit the area in years.

Unless someone was putting the squeeze on her. That would be the crime of the century! One that would not be left unpunished. He would see that justice was served, whether it was on a cracked plastic plate at Dooley's, or on Colin's bologna-spattered griddle.

8

"NO NEED TO CAST A SPELL on me, Emaline. I'm already as smitten as a schoolboy."

"This has nothing to do with you, Dooley," Emaline bit out, jolted by his abrupt appearance at her booth in the back of the café. She snapped the thin brown volume in her hands shut with a smack.

"A cryin' shame. A real cryin' shame."

She flashed daggers at him in the vain hope of driving him off. He continued to hover, however, openly curious about Aunt Verna's ancient book on astrology. It was her lunch break, the one time of the day when her boss usually left her alone because of the midday crowd. He reminded her of a nasty Humpty Dumpty as he teetered over the edge of the table. His slicked black hair accentuated the egglike shape of his head, and the thick waistline straining his black gabardine pants brought his center of gravity to the tippy center of his torso. If he were to fall her way, she'd suffocate within seconds, if not from his weight, from sheer nausea!

"So, what are you reading up on, Emaline?" he asked, his tone as slippery as his head.

"The stars, the planets," she mumbled vaguely, setting the book facedown in her lap out of sight.

"Maybe I'll join you." He rubbed his thick hands together as if plotting some sort of juicy rendezvous.

Oh, how she hated his invasions of her privacy. And it was so important that she find an antidote to the moonstruck curse. "Who will see to the customers?" She strained to see over the back of the booth, praying that some new faces had materialized since she'd buried her nose in the yellowed pages of ancient wisdom. Dooley, too, cast a look around the café. Unfortunately, Mondays were slow. Many of the locals who gathered here to chat skipped the first weekday to catch up on errands.

There were three customers total, all seated on stools at the orange counter: Evie Jo Kline, a classmate of Emaline's who clerked at the bank. Old Doc Fitzhenry, the town's semiretired veterinarian. Little Lillian Waters, Hollow Tree's tiny, middle-aged manicurist and daughter of Granny Lillian Waters, resident postmistress.

Mayor Carl Withers, who organized the annual Harvest Moon Festival was on hand, too, but he didn't count as a paying customer. He'd only stopped by to tack a bright yellow festival flyer to the bulletin board near the door.

"Maybe you should tend to Carl," Emaline advised.

"He's scurrin' up and down Main Street with those papers for tomorrow's celebration," Dooley said dismissively, propping his hand on the back of the opposite seat. He openly combed her with a lusty gleam in his mismatched eyes of blue and hazel. Aunt Verna often said he had all the signs of the evil eye: different-colored irises, eyeballs set close together and deeply in the head.

Emaline automatically slipped her hand under the table and crossed her fingers out of his sight to ward off misfortune, as she always did when he bored directly into her soul. She wondered if the superstitious café owner had ever spotted the evil eye in his own reflection. She doubted it. Milton Dooley could never accept an imperfection in himself.

The jingle of the front bell caused them both to turn their attention to the glass door. Emaline's heart fell as she realized there was no new distraction on the way in. Carl was stepping out into the late-morning sunshine. A glance at the thin gold watch on her wrist told her she had ten minutes left of her break. Dooley would stick like gum on her shoe for the next six hundred seconds. She began to count them off one by one in her mind. One thousand one, one thousand two . . .

Just as Dooley was about to slide into the seat with her, he lurched back up again. Something had obviously caught his eye on the street.

"It's him!" he blurted out hoarsely, jabbing a meaty finger at the front pane.

"Him who?" Emaline asked in feigned wonder. Naturally she already knew, even as she sprang from the booth to follow Dooley to the front of the café. Dooley's look of sheer disbelief could only mean one thing: John Monroe was paying them a visit. Emaline bobbed around the stout Dooley, peering out the window between the white lettering that fittingly read POT PIT from the inside.

"It's Jackson Monroe," Dooley muttered in awe, nearly tripping over his shiny black shoes and Little Lillian Waters as he grasped for the corner of the counter.

"He's dead," Little Lillian chirped, deftly pushing aside her cup and saucer with professionally trimmed and polished fingertips as Dooley's palm landed before her with a thud.

Dooley's chest heaved as he laboriously sucked in oxygen. All the diners and Emaline watched as his face reddened and the half circles of perspiration under the arms of his white shirt widened to huge crescents.

"I suppose I can see why the man easing off the motorcycle might be mistaken for my late husband," Emaline said, forcing a soothing calmness into her tone. To the diners, she knew his wiry form was every bit as broad-chested under his tapered royal blue shirt, his hipline lean and rock hard against his snug tan jeans. Even his brown boots greatly resembled Jackson's.

"What do you mean mistaken?" Dooley sharply interrogated.

"Well, most confusing is the helmet concealing his dark hair, of course," Emaline hastily informed him. "Yes, to the untrained eye, John could be mistaken for his brother." She held tough with a cocky grin under Dooley's suspicious glare. It was her first and only chance to sell Dooley, train his mismatched, evil eyes to see what she wished them to see.

"John Monroe?" Dooley repeated in puzzlement, eventually falling into a moody scowl. "That no-good rambler had a brother?"

"Jackson was a wonderful man!" Emaline cried in his defense, her smooth demeanor fraying at the edges. Her eyes darted out the window as John removed his helmet, his rusty hair gleaming in the sunshine as a welcome banner of deception. A sudden grunt by Dooley and a cry from Little Lillian drew her attention to the counter behind her. She whirled to find her boss lunging over the counter for the nearest saltshaker, nearly crushing the petite white-haired woman in his dive. Before Little Lillian could pummel him with her fist, Dooley had teetered back on his feet with unbelievable agility, swiftly shaking three dashes of the white grains over his left shoulder.

"Scared of a ghost, are ya, Milt?" Doc Fitzhenry taunted with a toothy grin.

"Shut up, old man," Dooley lashed out wildly. "Never hurts to take precautions."

"Enough salt on the floor to melt a sheet of ice," Evie Jo Kline remarked from the stool behind Doc. "Warding off bad luck only takes a pinch or so."

"Perhaps the hefty person needs a bit more, pound for pound," Little Lillian ribbed.

Emaline snapped her attention back to the window. Jackson was stepping up on the curb now, stalking across the sidewalk with long, purposeful strides. She shuddered at the thought of what could happen once he confronted them. Did he have another trick in mind, one similar to his engagement trap last night? What if the dam burst on his pent-up frustration? What if he knocked Humpty Dumpty down on his flabby gabardine butt? Her fingers instinctively reached for the pearly moonstone pendant hanging around her neck, squeezing it hard. Oh, if the moon had any forces in the light of the sun, now was the time, she pleaded.

"John, eh?" Unreadable emotions played on Dooley's pinched face as he carefully sized up the brother Monroe opening the door to his establishment. Ultimately Dooley seemed satisfied that he could keep the upper hand in this encounter.

"John Monroe, I'd like to introduce you to the owner of the Tip Top, Milton Dooley. Milt, this is Jackson's brother John, an attorney from Ohio." Emaline's heart hammered like crazy beneath her uniform pocket with the mock-hanky adornment as Jackson loomed silently over them. He made her wait several heartbeats, his features etched in stone, his eyes hidden behind the dark lenses of his steel-rimmed glasses.

In the end it proved to be Emaline who decided when the waiting was over. A smile crept into the corners of her mouth. All was well. He'd taken a blade to his face since her peek into the pantry early this morning. He was still willing to cooperate, even if he was attempting to hold her hostage at the moment!

Jackson caught her subtle wink. The small marital duel was over. In obvious surrender to his wife/fiancée he turned to nod curtly in Dooley's direction. Off came the glasses, which he stuffed into his shirt pocket.

"Another Monroe," Dooley sneered, his mismatched eyes shining as his mental gears churned. As fearful as he was of dueling with a spirit, he was obviously more than ready to tangle with the flesh-and-blood brother.

Jackson grasped Emaline's elbow firmly. "Let's take a lunch break together, Emaline. I have a surprise for you."

"Another one?" She flinched, struggling with her composure. "I'm already sitting in the last booth along the wall." She gestured toward the back of the café, taking a step in lead. "Can I get you anything to eat?"

"He'll get it." Jackson turned to face Dooley with a thin, fathomless smile. "This is his place. This is your time off." As Dooley blustered for an uppity reply, Jackson ordered black coffee and ushered Emaline down the narrow aisle between the booths and the counter stools.

Emaline eased back into the seat facing the front window. Jackson slid in right beside her.

"What will people think, you plastered against me?" she hissed in worry, a smile frozen on her face as the threesome at the counter fidgeted on their stools for a closer look.

"They'll think we're engaged, honey pie." He squeezed her knee under the table, causing her to squeak like a chatty doll.

"I haven't told any of them yet," she objected.

"That's why I'm here, sweet Emaline," he intoned in amusement, kissing her cheek for all to see. "I'm anxious to help you spread the news."

"Can't you let me handle this in my own way?" she beseeched.

"I'm sure you could top my funeral extravaganza with some sort of engagement announcement, wife . . . to be. But I can't risk letting you make any more plans on your own. It's dangerous to my health."

Emaline balked at the man beside her, her artificial smile straining with her patience. "You can't trust me? How can you, of all people, say that? After all I've done for you—"

"You've done more than your share, Emaline."

"Yes." She shook Verna's book of Romany wisdom at him before tucking it into the side pocket of her purse. "As the minutes tick by I search for the antidote. And do my duties here," she added, searching his face. Nothing. "I suggest you wake up and do what you must do, as well."

Oh, but how he was trying to do just that! With a lingering sigh, Jackson stared off into space. Quite accidentally he found his gaze suddenly locked in on Evie Jo, seated on the stool nearest them. She wiggled her fingers and other things in flirtatious greeting, her long sandy-colored mane flowing to her waist like a smooth strip of beach.

"She's nothing but trouble," Emaline whispered, keeping a stern, steady eye on her former classmate. "Never satisfied in school unless she bested me."

"I recall her trying to woo Jackson Monroe into her corner. At this very café, while I was remodeling the kitchen. Why isn't she waitressing here anymore?" he asked, noting her plaid skirt and tight white sweater. He turned back to Emaline to find her face nearly on her plate of toast. "You took her place, didn't you?"

"Yes," she mumbled in confession. "She clerks at the bank now."

"She's more industrious than I realized," Jackson mused.

"Dooley got her in," Emaline snorted. "Word around town is that he gave her a glowing recommendation."

"Who'd believe that scum bucket?"

"Dooley may be a lech, but he's considered a shrewd businessman by the other merchants."

Jackson was itching to ask Emaline why she didn't vie for the other job, but knew he'd be probing a wound already sore. Instead he lifted his hip off the vinyl bench and dug into his front pants pocket. Emaline's dark eyes widened as he produced a small velvet box.

"Is this my surprise, John?" she asked in open relief.

He could only imagine what she thought was up his sleeve! "A ring, Emaline, to help back up my sincerity." All eyes at the counter were on them as Jackson slipped the round diamond encircled with garnet chips on her finger.

"It's lovely, John!" she murmured in pleasure, holding out her hand, as the patrons slipped off their stools for a closer look. "If only..." she trailed off helplessly.

"Landed another man from the Monroe family, I see," Evie Jo noted, bending over the booth to eye the ring, her cheek brushing against Jackson's shoulder.

Dooley's shuffling feet interrupted their chat. "One coffee." He set a plate and cup and saucer down on the table with a thud. "Time's up, Emaline. It's back to work for you."

"But, I—" Emaline protested as the circle around her began to disperse.

"You go on ahead, Emaline," Jackson directed, easing his narrow hips out of the booth to give her passage.

She slipped her bottom across the bench, all the while gazing up at Jackson's determined expression. So he did intend to speak to Dooley! A tight hand on her purse, she marched down the aisle and around the counter, jamming her bag into a bottom shelf beside the napkin packages. She straightened up and rested her forearms on the counter beside Doc Fitzhenry, wondering what the men were saying. But the distance and the din of the jukebox that had kept her talk with Jackson private were camouflaging this conversation, as well.

"Emaline, service over here, please."

Very reluctantly Emaline cast an eye at the two farmhands at booth two and grabbed a fresh pot of coffee. She had a job to, no matter how much she despised it.

"Dismiss Emaline?" Dooley was guffawing as he twisted around in the cramped booth to watch his prized waitress fill coffee cups with proficiency. "You're daft, Monroe. What gives you the right to breeze into town and rearrange a satisfying arrangement? Your brother's dead and gone. So is any claim he had on Emaline."

"I'm not only Jackson's brother, but I'm Emaline's new fiancé," Jackson pleasantly informed the stout, arrogant man seated before him. "Just slipped a ring on her finger."

Dooley's jowls dropped in pure shock over the announcement. "So quick? Why, it just can't be."

The wheels were turning in the weasel's brain, Jackson realized. If only he could read his thoughts! At the very least he could exert some influence over the crafty café owner. Jackson rested his forearm on the table between them, deliberately curling his fingers into a massive fist for effect. Dooley kept right on grinning, but his eyes blinked with every flex of corded muscle.

"You, ah, talk to her about her job here, John?" Dooley asked, keeping his voice amazingly steady, as if he somehow had an ace of his own.

"I'm talking to you, man to man," Jackson spat harshly. Man to weasel was more like it. "No wife of mine needs to work."

"That may very well be true." Dooley bobbed his slicked head with mocking agreement. "You being a fancy lawyer from Ohio way."

"So, this will be the end of it."

Dooley wagged a thick, chiding finger with a smile. "I must insist you discuss this entire matter with your bride-to-be. For a second time, no doubt."

Jackson stiffened in his seat, struggling to disguise the fact that Dooley had hit a raw nerve. He'd hoped intimidation and muscle would throw the older, unfit man off balance. But Dooley was shrewed enough to turn the tables on him without skipping a beat. Dooley sensed Emaline was not cooperating with brother John's retirement plan.

"What's in it for you, Dooley?" he eventually asked, his flat, hard tone a perfect match for his eyes.

Dooley grimaced in irritation. "Let me warn you, John, I was not especially fond of your brother, Jackson. He was a cheating drifter who did some work here in the café. Why, the kitchen went up in flames shortly after he finished his handiwork."

"Are you accusing Jackson Monroe of arson?" Jackson asked sharply.

"Nothing so premeditated!" Dooley reared back slightly, despite his bravado. "The man is dead and buried, besides. He and I came to an arrangement of sorts before his passing," he intimated smugly.

News to Jackson Monroe! Who was simmering in a storm of rage across from him!

"Jackson was totally wrong for Emaline right from the start," Dooley rambled on with authority. He leaned back in his seat, lacing his fingers over his barrel chest. "I'm not convinced Emaline would be doing the right thing by parting company with me, especially for a second Monroe."

Jackson clenched his teeth as the other man spat out the proud Monroe name like a mouthful of sour wine. "You talk as if you have some claim to her."

"Hollow Tree Junction lays claim to all its local beauties," he replied smugly, casting a covetous look at Evie Jo, seated on a stool several feet away.

"But Emaline is different from the others," Jackson asserted, his eyes following Dooley's to the harder-looking young woman.

"Oh, indeed," Dooley agreed, his chest heaving to button busting proportions with his satisfied sigh. "The lovely Emaline needs a firm male to take charge. She is a ripe young woman who has known a man's touch. In a way I've filled that role, during her spell as a widow. Given her guidance, seen her down the straight path. My long-range plan has been quite successful. I've managed to keep her right here under my watchful eye."

"You seriously planned to marry her?" Jackson didn't try to mask the awe in his tone.

"Have since the funeral," Dooley affirmed, flashing yellowed teeth. "I certainly will not fire her, not after all the effort I've put into nurturing her. She's been rather warming up to me lately. Just this morning, she was poring over some book concerning the phases of the moon.

The harvest moon in particular is a big deal around these parts," he informed Jackson. "It's normally considered a bonus night of light for farmers harvesting their crops into the late hours. We here in Hollow Tree Junction use that night for a town celebration, rejoicing our fertile farmland, our fertile people."

"She wants me, Dooley," Jackson proclaimed intensely. "Get that through your thick skull. It's me and only me."

"Just for the sake of argument, let's say she does, John," Dooley surprisingly conceded. "Maybe with your youth and vigor you could best the better man. But I want you to know that beyond sentiment, there are other considerations involved in my relationship with Emaline."

Jackson felt he was on the verge of a discovery. "Considerations often mean cold cash," he ventured smoothly, determined to keep his temper in check.

"I'll bet you're a smart lawyer, perhaps shrewder than your savage wandering brother," he conceded with lift to his rounded shoulders. "Regardless, I wouldn't dream of tipping over the apple cart as it so profitably stands, John. If Emaline comes to me and says she wants everything out in the open for all to see, I'll be more than happy to oblige. Until then, I have me a waitress."

Jackson watched Dooley laboriously climb out of the booth and waddle down the aisle, greeting patrons on his way. It took Herculean strength to sit still, not to lunge forth and grab him by the shoulders and throttle cooperation out of him. It was Dooley's nature to be up to dirt. But just what connection he had with Emaline remained to be seen. Jackson certainly couldn't deck a man over a suspicion.

Dooley's mentioning the fire had surprised him. If Jackson recalled correctly, the blaze had happened a few weeks before he took off. He'd seen the charred kitchen. It had been an electrical short, having no connection whatsoever with the cabinets and countertops he'd installed. Dooley had tried to scatter the blame in many directions, from the plumber to the tiler to Jackson himself. Dooley had skimped on the remodeling job, leaving in the old wiring. His accusations had seemed hilarious at the time. And they'd had a heated argument to settle it, too.

Despite Colin's self-centeredness, it now seemed likely that Dooley was the far more dangerous of the pair.

His need for answers, for retribution, ate away at his insides. He wanted to cram justice down this bastard's throat. If he'd soiled his wife, Milton Dooley's next visit to the cemetery would be as the guest of honor.

WAS THERE TRULY no rest for the wicked, or for the allegedly dead?

Jackson tossed and turned in his bed into the night, submerged in dreams of Emaline, open roads of freedom and a combination of the two. But there was an insistent interruption that furrowed his brow, disrupted his blissful flight along the creamy shoulders of soft flesh and gravel shoulders of roadway.

It was a distinct tapping from somewhere on the other side.

His toes curled unconsciously against a tickle, his jaw tightened against the threat of a blade. A man was never truly safe in this world, especially not while in vulnerable slumber, specifically not while in the Holt house. He'd traveled so many miles to reach what he thought would be a safe haven from the storm, only to find himself consumed in a raging Gypsy fire. Who would next invade his quarters, cavalierly throw aside his bedcovers?

He rolled, he stretched, turned on his side, folding the pillow over his ear. Still, there was no relief, no halt to the invasion tapping away at his brain like a tiny steel hammer, drowning out all else.

Blast! Jackson bolted up in bed, the heels of his hands digging into his temples. Tap-tap-tap. His head spun in the dimly lit pantry as he struggled to get his bearings. The sound was real, coming from the direction of the room's only window facing the backyard. Moonlight streamed in through the lacy curtains drawn against the pane, pooling over the bed in a webbed design.

He sprang to his feet, a huge, bare predator except for white cotton briefs. He stalked across the cold, hard floor to investigate with a discontented rumble, ripping the lacy fluff of fabric away from the glass with a swat.

Fingers were hammering at his pane. Ten tiny, rounded nails were tapping like cool raindrops. He swiftly lifted the window a foot high.

"It is I, John," a hushed voice announced from the yard. "Emaline."

Jackson set back on his heels, blinking dumbfoundedly in the darkened room. Emaline had come to him? What luck. They hadn't had a moment alone since the café at lunchtime. After a supper honoring their engagement, her family had whisked her off to plan the wedding. What was she up to? Romeo's gig in reverse? Jackson's heart pulsated with hope. She wanted him. Now. Outside. In the cool grass.

She'd found a cure to her moonstruck curse! That was it!

"John?" the voice prodded urgently. "Are you there?"

Jackson dipped his head out into the night, vitalized by the cold air and her hot black eyes. "I'm here," he assured her huskily. She was a peaches-and-cream dream in her silky ankle-length negligee with flowing bed jacket. The light breezes had picked up both hems, giving her an ethereal look, as if she could float up to his waiting arms.

"It is I, Emaline," she repeated in a strained whisper.

"Yes, darling, yes," he swiftly acknowledged.

"And I, Margaret," a second voice added.

"And I, Lindy," a higher voice peeped.

"And I, Verna. And Puff-Puff," a voice and meow added respectively.

Jackson jerked forward in disbelief, banging his wide shoulder against the window frame as he angled out for a better look. His desires fell flat in a splat as he glared out at the semicircle of females behind Emaline, all shivering in their nightclothes. "Everybody?" he balked in a strangled voice.

"We didn't mean to disrupt your sleep," Emaline apologized tentatively under his ferocious glower, pushing her windblown hair out of her eyes.

"Perish the thought, ladies!" he bantered in hearty sarcasm. "Well, sorry that I can't come out and play. Not that some sort of preharvest Gypsy ritual isn't tempting . . ."

"Be serious, young man!" Margaret snapped. "Do you seriously think that a gaujo like me would be out in the autumn chill dressed in her nightgown if it were not for a . . . a reasonable reason!"

"Tell me all about reason," he goaded, resting a forearm on the sill.

"A prowler, John," Verna testified.

"In the house," Emaline affirmed.

"This very minute," Lindy whimpered without her usual bravado.

"A real prowler, not just the plumbing?" Jackson quizzed, adjusting to the peril.

"We were all in my room," Emaline began.

"Talking about the wedding," Lindy volunteered.

"On the third floor, you know," Verna validated.

"I know, ladies! I know!"

"We heard a noise down in the kitchen," Margaret hastily plunged in to report. "We thought it was you, perhaps raiding the refrigerator."

"But Lindy said you wouldn't," Verna noted.

"But he could have," Margaret tossed back angrily.

"Then we heard it in the parlor," Emaline continued.

"Then we heard it on the second floor," Lindy reported.

"So we snuck down the back staircase, through the kitchen and out the back door," Margaret finished. "We would've rapped on your door, but we were afraid he'd hear us."

"Getting you up is like waking the dead," Lindy retorted, stomping her foot in the grass.

"Oh, it's different with just the right tickle," Verna said knowingly, cuddling Puff-Puff as Emaline turned to glare at her in confusion.

"Stay here," Jackson broke into the feminine chatter as he heard a distinctive thump overhead. "You never know what you're walking into with a burglary."

"There is no such thing in Hollow Tree Junction," Margaret argued.

"I suppose you think it's a friend, Margaret," Verna admonished with a toss of her pink-rollered head.

Jackson rubbed his hands together in fiendish anticipation. Friend or foe, he'd soon know. Colin? Naw, he had the run of the place. Skulking wasn't his style. What if Dooley had come a-callin'? Maybe brother John had pushed his panic button. Jackson wanted nothing more than a concrete excuse to lay Mr. Tip Top out cold. "I'll handle this myself," he announced over the chattering, instantly drawing hushed sighs of relief.

"John?" Emaline's soft voice broke into his thoughts as he oriented himself in the darkened room.

Jackson dipped his head back out the window, speaking between gritted teeth. "Yes, Emaline?"

"Put your pants on first, before you save us."

"Very well, my beloved," he agreed on a ragged breath, ducking back inside.

"You'd think they were already married, wouldn't you, Verna?" Margaret murmured among the chirping crickets.

"Oh, my yes! Man and wife," Verna chortled back with much glee. "So masterful. Handsome is as handsome does."

Jackson grabbed his jeans from the back of the only chair. He didn't feel like a husband at all! Not with Emaline on the wrong side of the sill! Get her flat just once… She'd soon be singing a whole different tune about his pants! And she wouldn't stop singing until the moon turned blue!

Woe to the man invading this house.

Woe to the man interrupting his first night of undisturbed sleep.

Jackson stealthily climbed the back staircase on the balls of his feet, relying on his sense of touch and excellent hearing to guide him in the darkness. He'd snatched a rolling pin from the counter as he'd passed through the kitchen, and now gripped it at his side with steely fingers. The weapon was more for an initial show of intimidation rather than anything else. Any man from sea to shining sea who'd come in contact with Jackson's curled fist knew better than to try for a rematch.

The second floor was far from foreboding, even from the back of the hallway where Jackson now stood. A rosy glow streamed from Lindy's rosebud-papered room at his left. Farther down on the right, a radio hummed in Margaret's room. Verna's nest at the front of the house seemed black and silent.

Or so it seemed.

A distant thump and a circular splash of flash of light in Verna's doorway pinpointed the culprit. Jackson stalked down the passageway filled with photographs and flowers pressed behind framed glass. With his rolling pin raised, he snaked his free arm around the doorjamb to flick on the light switch.

"Stop, Monroe!" a thin, reedy voice cried out.

9

JACKSON PAUSED with the heavy wooden pin over his head, his jaw sagging in disbelief. "What the blazes are you doing?"

Colin Sinclair glared up at him from his kneeling position on the floor near the bed. "Searching for the book, of course! I've been scouring the house top to bottom for the ruddy thing."

"It's down in my room," Jackson told him. "I was going to bring it over tomorrow."

"Impeccable timing," the Brit responded, his narrow face twisting with scorn. "Especially considering that tomorrow would be too late. Oh, will you put that thing down." He gestured to the rolling pin. "You look like a psychotic chef."

Jackson set the pin down on the chair near the doorway. "Maybe you oughta sit down. You look sort of green."

Colin glanced glazedly around his surroundings. Jackson realized the man was seeing Verna's garish fuchsia-and-purple quarters in the light for the very first time. A huge canopied bed covered with shiny rose taffeta, shelves of clutter, mismatched dressers, heavy satin curtains that swept to the hardwood flooring made the lavender-scented room cramped and intimate.

No-man's land.

Colin edged his way toward Jackson, near the exit. "All my efforts for nothing."

"Had I known you were this desperate, I'd have brought the book over an hour ago," Jackson apologized in short temper. "What a stunt to pull."

"I told you I needed it."

"Yes, but in the middle of the night . . ." Jackson gave a puzzled shake to his auburn head. "This isn't your old smoothie style at all."

"I'm a man driven to the edge," Colin lamented bleakly, "a man running out of time."

Jackson's advice was brisk and to the point. "Look, pal, you gotta get out of here. Pronto."

"The ladies are upstairs," Colin assured him with a limp gesture to the ceiling.

"No they aren't, they—"

"Charlatan!" Verna burst into her own bedroom suddenly, punctuating Jackson's warning with the thrust of a fleshy arm. "Midnight marauder!" Her beady eyes focused on both men, a pair of boys caught with their hands in the cookie jar. Puff-Puff scampered in on her heels, wending her way around Jackson, pressing the length of her furry body against his calves.

"Not you, Colin," Margaret realized in dismay, stepping into the bedroom behind Verna. "Explain yourself this instant."

"Make it snappy, limey," Lindy joined in, her fears fading to impish glee at the sight of a squirming Colin Sinclair with dust rings on the knees of his green corduroy pants.

Jackson heaved a heavy breath as Emaline entered, making the feminine circle complete. They were surrounded. By a horde of angry women. In a room where spirits and magic floated in potpourri-tinged air. Near a bed boasting enough satin to create ten prom dresses.

"It is actually a misunderstanding between John and me," Colin attempted to claim with forced flair.

Jackson snorted in shock. The wily grifter was trying to deliver the blame on his doorstep like yesterday's newspaper: it was too late to do anybody any good. "This is your scene, pal. You take your medicine."

"I merely wanted a favor—"

"Favors in my boudoir, sir?" Verna choked in mortification.

"Certainly not!"

"You are a burglar, Mr. Sinclair," Emaline accused, her eyes shifting from Colin to Jackson with a flicker of confusion.

"Unless you've come to elope with Aunt Verna," Lindy slipped in craftily.

"You're wrong on both counts!" he asserted, wiping the last trace of compassion from Verna's puffy pink face. "I meant only to borrow something from the kitchen, I assure you."

"There are no kettles in here," Verna righteously pointed out. "No knives, no forks—"

Lindy cut in. "No snacks, either, unless you count some of the stuff in those jars on the shelf in the closet that I'm not supposed to know about until I've known the love of a good man." She drew her chin up, a mad twinkle in her eye. "Maybe we should make him taste some of that!"

"Enough, Lindy," Margaret chastised, casting a disapproving look at Verna. Jackson wagered that Verna's secret closet stock would be in a sealed box on the road by next garbage pickup day.

"I meant no harm," Colin explained in a sputter.

"What if I had been in slumber? In my dressing attire?" She asked the question with a brave tremor, unabashedly standing before all of them in the gown in question.

"I knew you were all on the third floor," Colin said, attempting to placate. "I merely wanted to borrow the book until dawn."

"What book? What are you rambling about?" Margaret cut in. "Explain yourself without further delay."

"Not tonight," he refused, bringing a round of feminine gasps of surprise and outrage. "I shall be taking leave for now, and will return first thing in the morn. I suggest you all go to your rooms and get some sleep," he added, eyeing Jackson with a significant lift to his gray brow. With a gesture of farewell, Colin edged out of the circle and disappeared.

"We can't let him get away!" Lindy cried, shaking a fist in protest.

"Do you suppose he was trying to court my favors in a veil of secrecy?" Verna pondered with a romantic lilt.

"Are you insinuating you have outdistanced me in the contest?" Margaret blurted out, letting her genteel guard down. "Surely you aren't so romantically foolish."

"Who knows..." Verna trailed off, her honey-colored complexion flushed. "He may have wanted to whisk me off secretly to the justice of the peace before he ravished me."

"He merely wanted a book," Margaret insisted.

"Perhaps you were too hasty in trying to corner him, John." Verna turned to Jackson with a chiding cluck. "I know you were trying to help, but you may have destroyed my chances for a romantic life with a renowned author and Old World gentleman."

"You ladies rapped on my pipes, remember?" Jackson began in reproach, clamping his mouth shut again when Emaline gave his arm a warning squeeze. "Good night," he declared in surrender, rounding the doorway with a wave.

Upon his return to the pantry, Jackson found Colin at his window, feet planted firmly in the safety of the backyard. "Trying it from the outside, this time?" Jackson taunted, leaning against the sill.

"Thank you for coming so quickly," Colin said with a sigh of relief.

"Your desperation was heart wrenching up there," Jackson mocked. "If you are indeed looking for pillaging or elopement material, I'm already pledged to another. I suggest you try the second story. They're crazy for you up there. I'll even dig out a ladder. As man of the house I'd love to unload . . . relinquish one of our more mature ladies."

"Damn you, Jackson!" Colin sputtered.

"Slow down," Jackson chuckled. He moved to the dresser and rummaged through the top drawer, quickly producing the book of potions. He tossed it to the window, where Colin grasped it greedily, pressing it to his chest.

"I suggest you show up first thing in the morning," Jackson advised, wandering back. "I'm trusting you, despite your efforts to involve me in your B and E attempt."

Colin shrugged his thin shoulders, a gleam lighting his eyes in the moonlight. "Guess I panicked, being trapped up there in that mausoleum. I owe you one for this, old chum." He shook the book in the air victoriously.

"Just be sure you come back tomorrow."

"I shall. Of course it will mean not sleeping a wink tonight," he declared in self-pity.

"Why should you be the exception!" With a grunt Jackson shoved the window down. Hard.

"IF YOU GIVE THAT CREEP even one muffin, I'll have a fit!" Lindy stomped around the parlor the following morning, indeed already in the throes of the sort of fit she was threatening to have.

"Seems harsh." Verna softened, pursing her red painted lips.

"He may be starving," Margaret chimed in, patting her sister-in-law's hand.

"Lindy is right this time," Emaline declared, marching into the room in her pink Tip Top uniform. One look at the pair of women seated on the sofa set the tone for the confrontation ahead. They were waiting for their intruder friend in their Sunday best, despite the fact that it was only a Tuesday! Verna, dressed in her flowing lilac organdy, her auburn hair long out of her pink rollers and curled in tight ringlets against her head. Margaret in her best yellow linen suit, with a string of white beads at her throat, her graying blond hair pulled back in a huge silver barrette.

What was a girl to do with them? With hands on hips, Emaline paced the length of the sofa. "Fools for love, the two of you!" She glanced over at Lindy near the front window to find her little sister rocking on her heels, her mouth curling with cynicism. Perhaps the pot was calling the kettle black, Emaline realized. Who was a bigger fool for a man than she herself? Pining away for a husband who left her behind, saving herself for him like a closed rosebud.

"Let's not judge Colin until we get our facts straight," Margaret proposed.

"John's gone to fetch him," Emaline informed them, drawing double hushed murmurs. "Please, Mother, Auntie, let's get this competition between the two of you resolved today."

Both women inhaled nervously.

"Does this mean I don't get to call the sheriff?" Lindy asked in disappointment.

"It most certainly does, young lady," Colin pronounced in a clipped tone, as he breezed in on Jackson's heels, a large portfolio tucked under his arm. If he noticed the frills on the sisterly rivals, he didn't make note of it. Not only was he dressed in his usual frayed baggy way, but he was wearing yesterday's dark green trousers and striped oxford shirt.

Colin tipped his gray head, sniffing the air. "No apple crumble cake today?"

"There's always time for a bit of the apple later on," Verna responded, patting her hair.

"I believe there will be feasting soon," he predicted with assurance.

Emaline met Jackson's level gray gaze with trepidation. Colin Sinclair was certainly back to his pompous, caustic self. Jackson shrugged.

Colin set his folder out on the coffee table before the women, and extracted the leather-bound book from inside his sweater.

"My potion guide!" Verna took the book in her plump hands, gazing up at Colin in confusion. "This is what you wanted last night? Why? Have you cast a spell of your own?"

The very idea openly galled him. "Certainly not! I do not believe in such things."

"Then why, Colin?" Emaline prodded impatiently, knowing the elder women would never be direct with their beloved. "We deserve some answers. In the clear, sharp way that we all know is your trademark."

"I'm sorry I have to behave in such a strange manner, but I had vowed to myself to keep my secret to myself until it was time." With a flourish he opened the portfolio on the table, revealing some sketches of a mouse in various settings.

"This looks like one of your picture books." Margaret leaned forward on the cushions with interest, leafing through the illustrated pages.

"I've been working on my latest series centered upon one of nature's lesser creatures for months now. Gypsy Gerbil is her name," Colin announced proudly.

"All of the secrecy, the locked doors, is because of your new idea?" Margaret queried, not quite understanding.

"What's so top secret about it?" Lindy asked, her arms folded across her chest.

"I was using your household for my research, and wanted all of you to act naturally," he explained. "If I had let on, I never would've gotten the genuine feel to the ways of the Rom."

"An animal of Romany heritage!" Verna cried in outrage, sliding her rear end forward on the sofa for a closer look. "It is one thing to have innocent creatures of the forests and jungles in your stories, but to make fun of my ancestors. This is heathen, this is spiteful. This is me!" she suddenly squawked. Her fleshy chin quivered, her painted red mouth fell open.

"Are we all in your stories?" Emaline asked.

"To certain degrees," Colin said, taken aback by the overall reaction. "Verna is the central gerbil."

"Oh, my stars!" Verna lamented, drawing a kerchief from her organdy bosom. "I am a mouse for the world to see!"

"A gerbil is a rodent," Colin clarified, bringing on a fresh round of wails.

Emaline rushed over to give her aunt a comforting pat on the shoulder.

"It isn't really you, Verna. It is your spirit. Sort of . . ." he trailed off lamely. "I never dreamt you would be offended. I thought you would be honored."

"You should've asked permission," Emaline charged.

"I wanted it all to be spontaneous! Can't you see? As you have suspected in the past, I had a long dry spell. Nothing I wrote seemed to spark. I came over here more and more for companionship—"

"And meals," Lindy cut in.

"Yes, I was hungry," Colin admitted between gritted teeth, "without a bean to my name. But gradually, you ladies began to inspire me—even Lindy with her tart tongue. After missing the mark several times, I sold this three-book idea with no trouble at all. My publisher is waiting for them as we speak. I was simply ecstatic when John told me about your book on potions. I thought you had those committed to memory, Verna. But to learn you had a book!" He raised his hands. "I simply had to have it. Which explains why, in sheer desperation, I broke into your home last night."

"You were not here to propose to me?" Verna asked between sniffles.

"Surely you weren't ever serious about me, Verna," Colin tsked. "I am a boring recluse whose idea of a good time is a short walk down the lane, a snifter of brandy before the fireplace."

"I most certainly was serious about you!" she confessed. "And all I was to you was . . . was research!"

"I love you, dear," Colin knelt beside the sofa, patting her hand.

"You do?" she asked in girlish hope.

He closed his eyes with a nod. "Like a lovely sister full of pep and ginger."

"Oh, damn you, you libertine." she howled in her hanky, snatching her hand from his.

"What do you want over here, Colin?" Jackson broke in, unable to contain himself any longer. Any of his women in tears brought out the fury in him. And for better or worse, he was bonded to the lot of them.

"I want everything to stay the same," he proclaimed matter-of-factly. "Why tamper with a jolly good arrangement?"

"Jolly good for you, perhaps," Margaret countered, standing up to face him sternly. "All the pretending."

"This silly triangular tryst between the three of us was nothing but harmless flirtation. It was not until Verna started to take an interest in me that you did, too."

Margaret blushed. "You've deliberately disguised your real motives, no doubt stringing us along for your own entertainment."

"If you thought I was pitching woo, I'm sorry. You ladies were entertaining yourselves," he declared with a haughty lift to his chin. "A contest with me as the prize. How common."

"We are not desperate spinsters waiting for a prize of a husband. And I think it unfair of you to submit this story based on Verna without her permission."

"It's already set. In the mail."

Verna rose in a lunge, ready for fisticuffs. Jackson stepped in and took hold of her. "Go home, Colin. Now."

"All right," he surrendered drearily. "Still, 'tis a pity to throw out the baby with the bathwater, sever our lovely friendship over so little."

"Get out, get out and never come back!" Verna shouted unmercifully.

Colin strode toward the door, pausing to turn with a grim look. "I shan't return uninvited. Never again." When no one objected, he exited.

Margaret dusted her hands together, a determined look on her face. "All right, John. Fill us in."

"I didn't know what he was up to," he claimed defensively, gently consoling the woman sobbing into his chest. No doubt they figured out how Colin got the book!

"Of course you're blameless," Margaret assured him with fond exasperation. "Obviously we need your legal advice again. What is our recourse after this heinous crime!"

"HOW DARE YOU behave like a lawyer?" Emaline admonished him in the kitchen five minutes later, shutting the door for privacy.

"John is a lawyer, right?" he pointed out practically, tracing a finger along her collarbone.

"I didn't expect you to practice law!"

"I am doling out sensible advice," Jackson contended. "I didn't get involved in any legalities, I simply stated that it's in the ladies' best interest to cool their jets about Colin. There will be plenty of time for action, whether it be legal or conjugal."

"This deception is out of control." She paced the floor. "You are out of control."

"Let's call it quits, then," he suggested eagerly. "Go throw some things in a satchel, wife. I'll fire up the Harley. We'll explain the whole crazy mess to them in a long-distance phone call sometime tomorrow."

"You said you'd never leave."

"Not without you."

She whirled on him in accusation. "That's how it began the last time. Then poof, you were gone!"

"Not this time," he gruffly contended, drawing closer for an embrace. She was as stiff to the touch as the ladder-back chairs nearby.

"You are deliberately rumpling me," she huffed, slipping out of his arms.

"Yep." Jackson's greedy eyes roved down her pale pink dress accented with the stiff white apron and phony half hanky peeping out of the breast pocket. "I love a girl in uniform," he crooned. "A tip-top gal. What do you say we go upstairs to the tub? I can play the wayward sailor and you can play the curvy yellow-haired mermaid, giddy to guide me back home through dangerous waters."

"I have to go to work," she reminded him crossly. "And I don't think my job is a funny matter."

"Well, it's a merry subject today, wife," he murmured in her ear, taking a juicy nibble at her lobe. "I called Dooley and told him you'd be off, due to harvest celebration preparation."

"You did?" she gasped in amazement.

What did Jackson read in her onyx eyes beyond the uncertainty? Hope? Admiration? What the hell did it mean?

"What did Dooley say?" she asked hesitantly.

"What could he say?" Jackson grinned with a shrug, enveloping Emaline's now pliant body in his arms. The jerk had been quite blunt and to the point. Fiancée or no, Emaline had better be back to work Wednesday morn. But she wasn't going back. Not ever. Jackson had a lot of conquering ahead of him tonight. And making love to his sweet wife would be the best conquest of all.

10

"AH, THE LOVEBIRDS are at it again!"

Emaline broke away from Jackson as Verna entered the parlor on a trill. "Oh! Aunt Verna, we were just—"

"No need to explain, *posh*," Verna lovingly chided. "John is a passionate man who has declared his troth. An honorable suitor who has presented you with such a beautiful engagement ring." She took Emaline's hand and passed her palm over it for the umpteenth time. "Diamonds and garnets," she gushed. "I can feel the warm energy flowing into my hand. Energy that should be fulfilled with vows of marriage."

"Emaline feels like my wife already," Jackson confided with satisfaction, massaging Emaline's shoulders from behind. "We attorneys are extremely hot-blooded beneath our blue serge suits. We believe in quick action."

Verna released Emaline's hand. "We should do the cards before the picnic."

Emaline's heart hammered as Jackson's fingers kneaded her muscles and Verna needled her brain. "I don't think John wants his fortune told again, Auntie," she declined with force.

"No matter, Emaline. I am so truly puzzled by John's fortunes that I've decided to concentrate on you." Verna pivoted on her patent-leather heel. "I'll just get my deck."

"We can't let her do it," Emaline said frantically. She tried to break free of Jackson's grip, but he held her still, his fingers digging into her stiff muscles.

"What harm can it really cause?" he challenged.

"Can you stand there and deny that her tea-leaf fortunes have been false?" She wrenched free of his grasp and spun to face him. "The boomerang and the scissors. Then the wig and the cat. Oh, yes," she fumed, "Lindy told me about that second reading."

Jackson chuckled. "Yeah, the cat really had Auntie going."

"Can you deny she's on the right track?"

"No, actually I'm rather impressed with her accuracy," he conceded. "An interesting run of luck."

"All right, children," Verna interrupted, floating back into the room. "Sit down on the sofa, Emaline. What would you prefer, the cross or the lucky thirteen?"

"Neither one," she said, glumly sitting down with her aunt.

"Lucky thirteen it is!"

Emaline reluctantly shuffled the deck and cut it in two with her left hand. Just as she was fanning them out into a half circle on the coffee table, Margaret appeared in the doorway.

"Don't tell me you're fussing with those now," she said. "I need help loading the sedan! There's the chicken salad, the fruit tray. And the last of the hanging pots for the bandstand, too. The mayor will be starting his welcome speech without his chrysanthemums, if we don't hurry."

"We're coming now, Mother," Emaline assured, popping to her feet.

"You haven't turned over a single card!" Verna complained, anxiously eyeing the fan.

"I know," Emaline murmured with a playful grin of relief.

THE PARK was already full of Hollow Tree revelers when Jackson eased the family sedan to the curb a block off Main Street a short time later. He went about the task of unloading the gear from the trunk, a bouncy Lindy at his side, coaxing him into the potato-sack race that she and brother Jackson won last year. Jackson gazed out at the rolling yards of grass dotted with swaying trees, a yellow-and-white-striped tent and a cluster of picnic tables. It all brought back sweet memories of homemade food, lively music and a host of traditional picnic games. The group of chattering females with him had been the closest he'd ever come to hearth-and-home living. If only he could remain the beloved John forever. If only they'd fussed over the simple Jackson Monroe with such compassion.

Then there was the town itself. He had to respect Hollow Tree citizens for the friendship and loyalty most of them shared. He scanned the laughing crowd in perplexity. Surely they wouldn't have judged Emaline too harshly for losing her man to the road, would they? She'd certainly gone to a lot of trouble to fool them. Looking at them now. . . . It was simply hard to believe that they would've mocked her.

Emaline stood on the curb hugging a bowl full of chicken salad and watching Jackson take things out of the trunk. His body was so strong, his motions so fluid. He looked more like himself every day, dressed in a red flannel shirt and faded jeans, the wind tousling his rusty hair. She had to admit with his new blond hues and whisker stubble, he was a cross between the brothers. She sensed the end was near. The truths would soon be faced. She shivered in spite of the warm breeze. Jackson was going to seduce her tonight, and she didn't know how she could say no—especially to her own desires. Her emotions were tied in knots, her body coiled, ready to spring at the graze of her handyman's fingertip.

"John's ready to hit the sack," Lindy chirped.

Emaline's head snapped to her sister, leaning lazily against the side of the car in a slogan T-shirt and blue shorts. It was almost as if the little *poshrat* could read her mind sometimes. She was dangerous enough with the tea leaves, cards and crystal ball!

"The potato-sack race, Emmy," she explained. "Just like Jackson and me last year."

"Just like it," Jackson chimed in, shutting the trunk with a heavy-handed thump.

"First the mayor has to make his dopey speech," Lindy grumbled, tossing her black tresses over her shoulders. "Then we'll have to eat."

"Hurry with that last pot, Verna," Margaret called back as she started across the lawn. "He's up on the bandstand testing the microphone."

"Coming, coming." The pair hurried off into the crowd with their chrysanthemums.

"I suppose we have to unload this food at the tent," Lindy declared impatiently, waving to a group of teenage girls giggling under an oak tree.

"You go on ahead and we'll take care of it," Jackson said with a shooing gesture. With a cheery wave, Lindy was off.

"We could've used the extra hands," Emaline reproved softly.

"That's the last thing I need tonight." Jackson hovered over her as he balanced the cooler on his thigh. Emaline was fragile porcelain in a full-skirted dress of orange polished cotton, her lustrous hair flowing honey down her back. She looked as though strong hands could snap her in two. Oh, how deceiving appearances could be. "You, uh, prepared to blast that old moon curse into green-cheese bits?"

"About that, sweet baby..." Emaline stared up at him with a pleading look.

"No cure for the curse, huh?" Jackson growled as Emaline shook her head, staring down at her shoes. He glared off into the horizon, thinking of other trying times in the past when he'd jumped on his bike and started driving toward the setting sun. He wouldn't do it this time. Not to Emaline. Not to himself.

"Are you angry?" she softly asked her shoes.

"Not angry. Just hungry, for you, wife." Jackson set the cooler down on the boulevard and cupped her chin in his hand, drawing her dark eyes to his. "Maybe I haven't given you a lot of reason to believe in me up till now, but please, Emaline, help me save our marriage. Let me love you the way I so badly want to."

"We are doomed if I do."

"We are doomed if you don't," he returned huskily. "Think about it. What have we left with all the fences between us?"

Emaline felt an indescribable sense of loss as Jackson's hand fell from her face. Without another word, he grasped the cooler again and headed for the tables.

"Why, I never in a million years," Verna huffed an hour later as they munched on their potluck feast.

"What's the matter?" Margaret asked from the opposite end of the picnic table.

"Colin the cur has had the audacity to show up at the festival. How dare he after his terrible philandering behavior?"

"No one will speak to him," Margaret predicted, twisting on the wooden bench to eye the raggedly dressed Brit in his green cords and gray sweater. "He'll forever be the outsider. More corn, John?"

"No thank you," Jackson declined, wiping his face with his napkin. The paper scratched against his stubbled skin roughly, reminding him of his goals. He hadn't shaved since yesterday and would not shave again.

"Women are flocking around Colin," Emaline noted with a gasp of surprise. "Now, why . . ."

"Go see why, Lindy," Verna ordered, jabbing a plastic fork toward the cur in question.

"I already know why," Lindy reported, unusually subdued. "My friends were talking about him. It seems that all the older ladies, single and married, want to be in one of his books, under the skin of any animal except a pig. They think Auntie is a darn fool for complaining. Colin may even end up with a key to the city before the first flake flies."

"Well, how on earth did they ever find out about my gerbil predicament?" Verna speared a cube of watermelon, popping it into her mouth.

"I may have mentioned it to Miss Talbot when she came in for her dozen roses this morning," Lindy feebly confessed, bringing on a round of disapproving groans. "Well, gee! You don't have to be so mean."

"That might never have leaked out," Margaret chastised, raising a paper cup of punch to her lips for an angry slurp. "Colin is so removed from the townsfolk."

"Well, she asked for a crystal reading, and nothing came up in the glass. We sat there awhile waiting. She asked why Verna was scolding the robins out back. She wondered why you were banging pots in the kitchen. Guess it just slipped out."

"Slipped out to that blabbermouth!" Verna fumed.

"Face it, Verna, there are few stones unturned in Hollow Tree Junction," Margaret said practically, smiling at John. "I know it may be difficult for you to understand, coming from the city. But there are virtually no secrets around here."

Jackson shook his tarnished auburn head in doubt. "I suspect there are a few scattered hither and yon, Margaret."

"The sack race is about to start," Lindy broke in, fidgeting to escape. "C'mon, boomerang boy."

"Excuse me, ladies," Jackson said. "If anything else, I am a man of my word."

"Such a good sport," Verna judged, watching the pair trot off toward the game area beyond the swings. "Isn't he a good sport, Emaline?"

"Yes, he's trying to be," Emaline conceded wistfully, rising to collect the scattered paper plates and cups. Why didn't he go all the way and clear up the whole sad state of affairs? "I'm going for a walk," she announced with a sigh. "I need time to think."

"What is wrong with you tonight?" Verna prodded later into the evening, regarding her niece with concern. "Everyone's been commenting on your long face, Emaline. I knew we should have read your fortune before leaving the house."

"Aunt Verna, about the moonstruck curse . . ." she began, gulping hard.

"Stop thinking about your father, Emaline," Verna said. "Just because this is the fifteenth anniversary since he and your mother . . ."

"Why, Verna Holt, that is no one's business but mine!" Margaret scolded furiously. "And stop blaming that stupid curse!"

"Is there a cure for that lovers' curse, Aunt Verna?" Emaline asked, anxiety clouding her features.

Verna paused in contemplation. "Not that I know of," she admitted. "But why spoil such a lovely evening with such talk?"

"Evenin', ladies," Milton Dooley greeted, tipping the straw hat on his slicked black head.

"Evenin'," Emaline returned coldly, taking in his loud pink shorts and bright yellow shirt. He looked like an Easter egg.

"Where's the boyfriend of yours, Emaline?"

"He's off with Lindy, competing in some of the contests," she told him levelly.

"Missed you at work today. You gonna marry this man?"

"She most certainly is, Mr. Evil Eye," Verna interrupted staunchly, crossing her fingers behind her back.

"Is that what you ladies call me?" he tsked.

"You do indeed have the evil eye, sir," Verna maintained. "'Tis no matter now, since Emaline's new husband will be supporting her. She'll no longer be dealing with the likes of you."

His mismatched eyes glinted with fury. "We shall see."

"What on earth did that horrible man mean, Emaline?" Margaret asked, patting her daughter's shoulder as Dooley skulked off. "Is there anything I can do?"

"John will have to save me, Mother," she told her quietly.

Jackson saw Dooley bobbing over Emaline from across the park. The sight of her cringing under him caused him to fumble the water balloon toss, drenching his partner's shirt.

"Oh, for pity sake, we could've won!" Lindy squealed angrily, pulling her wet T-shirt away from her skin. Their only other opponents at this point were Evie Jo Kline and a hand from the Jenks farm. Because they were the last couple dry with their balloon intact, they were declared the winners.

Jackson took the grumbling Lindy by the elbow and led her back toward the tables. "Look, kid, we won three games out of five. You have a pen and pencil set, a box of canning jars and a ceramic spoon rest decorated with the face of George Washington."

"I especially wanted to beat that jerky Evie Jo," Lindy whined. "Emaline hates her more than ever now that she works at the bank."

"How'd she get that job and not Emaline?" Jackson asked as they wended their way through the crowd.

"Evie Jo was at the bank a couple of weeks before Emaline came home to say she was workin' at the Tip Top. Guess she took the only job she could get."

"Do you know anything else? Anything that could help me out, kid?"

Lindy paused in her tracks amid a group of children, her expression as open and innocent as theirs. "I don't know what you mean, Jackie. But if I did know something, I'd tell you."

"I know, I know," he assured her, winding an arm around her shoulders.

When they reached the table, Lindy displayed her loot for all to see. Verna admired the spoon rest, Margaret admired the jars, and Lindy laid claim on the writing tools while she had the chance.

"C'mon, wife—to be," Jackson added after an extended pause. "The band is tuning up and I want to dance the night away with you."

Jackson hovered over the table, extending a hand to her. Emaline felt an exhilarating flutter in her stomach as his eyes greedily roved the length of her body. He wanted far more than to dance the night away. He remembered full well that once swaying in his arms, she was a goner every time!

"Sure you have enough energy for this?" Emaline asked, as Jackson guided her to the brick apron in front of the white octagon-shaped bandstand. "I mean after all of those games with Lindy?"

In reply Jackson twirled her around him, causing both her shiny cotton dress and mouth to flare in surprise. He yanked her back gently, his red shirt and blue jeans merging with her orange dress in flaming color. A few onlookers applauded their stylish step. Evie Jo Kline blew him a flirty kiss. Dooley's evil eyes bored through the pair. Lindy and her friends smirked behind their ice cream cones. Other couples began to move onto the smooth bricks, among them Colin Sinclair. It soon became evident that he knew a step or two. And the good ladies of Hollow Tree were lining up for the pleasure of dancing with him.

"Mother and Auntie will be crushed," Emaline fretted as the band struck up in a lively beat.

"Emaline, I know they're important to you, but I'm your family, too. And," he added huskily, "I need you more right now than the whole blasted town combined."

Emaline nodded in affirmation, allowing Jackson to steer her in a quick step number.

Many more townsfolk stepped forward to take part in rounds of square dancing and polkas. Numerous eyes were on Colin and his bevy of fans, but Jackson knew many were focused on John Monroe. Emaline's diamond sparkled on her finger as they twirled their way through the throng of dancers. If the murmurs could be believed, many actually thought that Emaline would eventually hitch up with Milton Dooley. Pangs of guilt over his flight pinched his heart; violent emotions over Dooley's game churned in his stomach.

When the music slowed down to romantic ballads, Jackson was ready to slow down. When Emaline inched closer, drawing her arms around his neck, he knew he was going to be saved for certain this night. Jackson molded his hands around Emaline's minuscule waist, shuddering as she grazed her nails through the small hairs trailing his hairline. They rocked slowly together in the swooning crowd, tucked away together in their own secret world.

Jackson's heart drummed in his chest as his eyes fell to the gap between them and he caught a glimpse of creamy breasts inside her bodice. She was wearing no bra. His lungs filled and emptied, heaving in sync with the creamy mounds he so wanted to touch. His hands ever so surreptitiously glided to the small of her back, pressing her into him. Her eyes widened as she connected with his slightly bulging pants.

"You're giving me ideas," he whispered into her hair.

"I can tell," she said with kittenish softness.

"If you say no to me tonight, I will be sorely compelled to tear down Hollow Tree Junction with my bare hands, nail by nail."

"I've given it a lot of thought, and I don't think I can say no," she breathlessly confided, clinging to him.

"Let's get out of here," he murmured in her ear as he scanned the crowd. "We'll just glide over to those high bushes edging the bandstand. No one will ever miss us."

Emaline allowed Jackson to lead her out of the crowd and around the gazebo. It was past eleven o'clock, and people were still scattered across the park, some carrying tired children to the sidewalk, others eating, drinking, embracing in the shadows of the huge old trees. Though it was dark, the moon had turned night into day, bathing the earth in a silvery glow.

"There's Mother, Verna and Lindy by the sedan," Emaline observed. "Hey!"

"Yes, we're leaving," Verna announced as they approached. With a grunt, she hoisted the cooler into the trunk.

"You should've let me do that," Jackson protested, joining her at the back of the car.

"Nonsense," she replied. "We Holt women are capable. We are glad Emaline has her man, but we need no English gent to make our home complete."

"Sorry about Colin," Emaline sympathized.

"We shall survive," Verna trilled with false bravado, allowing Jackson to set the picnic basket in beside the cooler and close the lid. Only Emaline noted that he'd pilfered the blue-and-white-checkered tablecloth as he reached for his leather jacket.

"We're going for a walk, ladies," Jackson announced as Margaret stood by the driver's door with the key ring in hand.

"Very well," she acquiesced, even more somber than usual.

As they piled into the sedan, Jackson stepped up on the curb, one hand waving, one hand clinging to his hidden treasure.

"I suppose that tablecloth is supposed to be our bedding," Emaline guessed as Jackson smugly tucked it under his sinewy arm.

Jackson lifted a rakish brow. "And why not? We are about to feast in each other, my darling. The prodigal husband has returned, so let's break open the bodice and celebrate."

Alone, but still a part of night, the festival, the land. They walked arm in arm along the near-deserted roads, as if their destination was a mystery as it had been the first time. Before long they were between the park and home at the Withers farm, in the same freshly harvested cornfield where they'd sated their passions last year. The revelers were a distance from them now, only traces of the music from the bandstand wafting overhead in the gentle autumn breezes. They couldn't have been guaranteed more privacy in a hotel room.

Jackson snapped the checkered tablecloth over the moist, tilled earth, then turned to gaze down at Emaline, who promptly flinched beside him. "Don't be frightened, Emaline."

Emaline's breath caught in her throat as he regarded her tenderly. How did he always manage to surprise and stimulate? "Jackson..."

Jackson squeezed the fingers she'd set upon his chest. "Good start, wife—you've called me by my given name."

"It will be all right, won't it?"

"It always was before," he chuckled softly, pressing his mouth to her forehead. "The moon is our lucky charm, Emaline."

"No," she argued.

"Regardless, the most powerful force right here and now is our love," he murmured gently but firmly, sidestepping even a short lecture on superstitious nonsense.

"I love you, sweet baby, I always have."

"You are trembling in my arms, wife," Jackson said softly. "There is nothing to fear, from me, the powers that may be, from the town, from Dooley. I am your lover and your protector and shall always be."

Emaline fought back tears. Jackson Monroe had changed. He was now the man she'd always dreamed of, one who would cherish her forever and ever. He would make it all right. "I trust you, Jackson," she finally cried out, eagerly accepting his crushing lips to hers. His tongue delved into her mouth, tickling and teasing her in much the same way he'd been doing in public of late. But these kisses weren't stolen appetizers. They were a prelude to flaming union between man and wife.

Emaline could feel herself relaxing, her limbs languid as she melded into him. He was barely touching her, she realized. It was she who was clinging, digging her fingers into his solid shoulders. She was exerting her feminine prerogative, revving her own desires into flaming frenzy. And he was loving every minute of it.

"What's your rush?" he teased as they broke the kiss, his hands alight on her back.

But Emaline wasn't fooled. His urgency was equal to hers in every breath. "What's the delay?" she countered in a moan.

"When your knees quake from passion only, I shall know you are really ready," Jackson explained softly in her ear. "It's been a traumatic year for you, Emaline. Though I've been tempted to force this moment, I feel differently now that it's arrived." He worked on the buttons of her bodice with clumsy fingers. The fumbling stopped, however, when his hand slipped into her gaping dress, weighing one cushiony breast, then the other in his palm. His fingers skimmed up, drawing her dress off her shoulders to expose her upper torso to the night. Clasping her arms, he dipped his head to her nipples, grazing them with his tongue in a lingering feast. Cool air rushed over her fevered skin, sending hot-cold flashes coursing through her system.

"Mmm . . . I've missed you, sweet baby." Emaline began to unbutton his shirt, tugging it out of his waistband, casting it off to the side. Anticipation for the sizzling journey ahead caused her to fumble as she unbuckled his belt and unzipped his jeans.

Jackson watched her as she worked, his voice steeped in lusty pleasure when he said, "Are you ready, Emaline?"

Emaline looked down at his pants, riding open on his hipbone, and moaned a deep, low, animal sound.

"My wanton wife." With eyes sheened in passion, he reached down to her thighs, drawing up the skirt of her orange dress. Emaline quivered as his roughened fingertips grazed her silky legs. Jackson dropped to his knees before her, pushed aside her dress and began placing featherlight kisses on her abdomen. With his first show of forcefulness, his hands suddenly invaded her panties, greedy fingers combing through her silken curls.

Emaline was already damp with anticipation when he plunged a finger inside her, skimming and sliding, rubbing her into sweet oblivion. She squeezed his shoulders, arching and writhing into the waves, her head tossed back in the wind like a corn silk tide, her skirt billowing high at her waist. She soon came in a trembling rush, collapsing against his kneeling figure. Jackson caught her has she fell, and together they rolled onto the tablecloth.

Jackson peeled her rumpled dress off her body. Emaline tugged at his pants, raising a chuckle from her beloved when she realized that she'd have to remove his boots first.

"You should've done this yourself right away," she grumbled, rising to her knees to gain leverage. She was completely bare herself, save for her sandals.

"I was busy entertaining you before," he claimed guilelessly as she grasped at one heel, then another. "Look, I'll do your feet if you do mine. The shoes work out just like the sex, wife. Sharing means so much." Jackson frowned as Emaline threatened to pitch the boot into the distance. "Don't you dare—I can't limp home on one heel."

Soon all feet were bare and Jackson's pants were heaped atop both boots. Jackson rolled onto his back, his bronzed body gleaming in a bath of moonlight. His arm curled around Emaline's perspiration-slicked back, drawing her over him. Jackson was rip-cord tense as she sprawled across his body with roaming hands. She skimmed over his hair-dusted chest, pressing into the rigid plane of muscle. As an experienced wife, she recognized this as a signal of his urgent need. "I love you, sweet baby," she sighed in his ear with a shiver.

Jackson pressed her head to his, kissing her slowly, languorously. He'd brought her over the edge first to provide the security she so desperately seemed to need. Now he really wanted to participate completely in the flight.

The mingling scents of the damp soil, the crisp autumn air and the beguiling fragrance of Emaline filled his nostrils as they tossed and tussled, wallowing in their physical reunion. Their fingers forged in frank exploration, touching, feeling, reacquainting. Emaline's smooth skin rubbed his limbs in strokes of velvet, swiftly driving him into frenzy. He kissed her harder, his fresh beard digging into her tender complexion. She lifted her face a fraction, nipping at his throat and nipples. When she moved to shift position he clamped his hands to her waist.

"Don't go, Emaline . . ." It was a plea, it was a command. Jackson had waited eight months and he could wait no longer. Lightning bolts of desire lanced his body, leaving his every fiber rock hard with need. Emaline moved to straddle him. With greedy hands she tucked his swollen shaft into her petaled folds. She began to rock over him, swallowing him deeper and deeper until he thought he could climb inside her forever. Jackson urged her on, pumping her waist, kneading her tight buttocks with his long fingers. They picked up a rhythm, blanketed by their whirlwind of passions and a silvery bath of moonlight.

If he could bring her around again with him . . . it would be perfection. He came in a spurting explosion, his body racking with a series of tremors. Emaline shuddered in climax as well, her heart pounding uncontrollably as she fell limp on his chest.

Holding her close, Jackson shut his eyes. Streaks of light flashed across his lids. When he opened them, he saw more of the same in the sky, in all colors of the rainbow. "Did we do that?" he asked, raising himself up on his elbows.

Emaline's eyes danced merrily as she lifted her chin from his chest, laughing. "They added fireworks to the celebration this year, sweet baby."

"Ah, I see."

"Gaujo fool," Emaline teased.

"You are the fool, Gypsy," he growled, stroking her spine. "There was nothing to fear from the harvest moon curse. Nothing at all."

They rested in each other's arms for a spell, sated, relieved. Finally, Emaline raised her head from Jackson's chest, eyeing him intently.

"What is it, wife?" he asked gruffly, halfheartedly cracking an eye open.

"Great sex doesn't solve everything."

"It was spectacular sex." His deep chuckle rose to a yelp with a swat of her hand on his thigh. "I'm sorry, I just wanted to blot out the other, just for a little while."

"So, are you finally ready to confess, Jackson? Ready to make retribution?"

Jackson was on his feet in a flash. Moonlight shimmered on every contour of his bronze nude body, accentuating every angle, every ripple of muscle. Emaline looked up at him from the ground, becoming unglued in the shadow of his warrior stance. The power of the world seemed behind his curling fist. "You, wife, are pulling all the strings now. I have done all I can with your limited confidences. It is up to you to tell me the whole story."

Jackson yanked Emaline to her feet. He didn't mean to frighten her, but he couldn't think down there, the scent of her enveloping him in a sensual cloud. And think he must. Finally, he was going to get the answers he needed. "How is Dooley threatening you, wife?"

"You're squeezing my arm," Emaline cried.

"Not hard. Just enough to still you."

"He's holding your debt over me, Jackson. Who on earth did you think would be left responsible?"

"What are you talking about?"

"The fire at the café," she spouted in frustration. "Dooley estimated the damage at seven thousand dollars—"

"Are you mad, woman?" Jackson roared. He threw his arms into the air, releasing her in a stumble. "That fire was caused by faulty wiring. It didn't concern me."

"He said he discussed it with you before your death, and you took the blame."

"We discussed it, all right," Jackson acknowledged, "but one look at the damage told me it was an electrical fire. Oh, he tried to swindle me out of some dough, but the counters and cupboards I installed certainly weren't a hazard. Remember me telling you?"

"I knew he was fussing while you worked, but you never told me a thing about his fire scheme!" she charged.

"Oh," he managed in concession, putting the brakes on his runaway temper. "I was playing the protector, trying to shield you," he recalled. "But how could you believe me to be so dishonest?"

"I wasn't very keen on you after you first took off," she righteously explained. "And you did leave right after the fire. And most important, he produced your signed promissory note. Had it right there at the funeral."

"No wonder he came to my send-off!" He paused in sudden realization. "So you must've buried me out of pride in the first place, just like I thought!"

"I don't know why you're still harping on it, but yes, I did!" she confessed indignantly. "We would've been humiliated to lose a second man!"

"And Dooley, believing that I was really dead, set out to extort you."

"Seems so," she agreed, biting her lower lip in fury. "I thought the funeral would end my troubles, but it was only the beginning. Dooley threatened to call the sheriff if I didn't make the note good. Mother and Verna would've found out and forever rubbed in your dishonest behavior. I feared they'd eventually discover you weren't really dead, too. Why, I might've been blamed for your escape. Whether you were dead, or a deserter, or honest or a crook, you just seemed to worry me to a frazzle, Jackson Monroe!" she ended in an exhausted rush.

"Why didn't you give him the money I sent you, instead of taking him on day after day?" Jackson wondered.

"I figured you sent it to settle the debt, but he didn't want money. He wanted me. Said he'd take two thousand off the seven if I worked it off at the café. Evie Jo had just moved over to the bank position. I decided not to fight him. If the police eventually tried to hunt you down, they'd have probably found you. What an I-told-you-so I'd have gotten then—with you in the clink!"

"This only happened because you didn't believe in me."

"Believe in a husband who took off?" she shot back, her black eyes flashing.

"Touché," he relented, rubbing the back of his neck.

"Touché better mean sorry," she sniffled. "I've been workin' my tail off to save our reputation."

"It sure explains how Evie Jo got the bank job," Jackson theorized, reaching for Emaline's orange frock, rumpled in a heap with his pants. He halfheartedly smoothed it, gallantly holding the bodice open for her. She stepped into it, stiff as he buttoned her up. He swiftly began to pull on his own clothing, tossing Emaline her panties when he found them tangled up in his shirt.

"You think Dooley got her the job so he could get a forged note?" she finally asked in quiet fury.

"I think he was searching hard for a way to snare you after you announced my death, and probably decided that open position at the bank would be a good opportunity for both of them," he speculated, pulling on his boots. "Dooley's no genius, but he's a greedy opportunist."

The entire picture was suddenly clear to Emaline. "No wonder Evie Jo's been snickering at me all these months!"

she sobbed, covering her face. "My life's a mess. I'm a mess, too. Just look at my dress, all wrinkled. And I'm freezing out here in the night."

Jackson tucked her inside his leather jacket, drawing her close. Emaline's soft sobs were the only sound in the field for a time. Pity and anger began to churn in Jackson's stomach, as the gravity of the situation settled in. "I knew I'd have to earn your trust again, but I just never guessed how completely."

"I just couldn't believe you didn't settle this thing the moment you arrived. Then you let me go off to work...."

"I begged you to talk to me and you would not," he reminded her.

"You're always bragging about your honest nature. Well, I wanted absolute proof of your character. Then you just hung around, being the favored John..." she trailed off in hurt.

"I couldn't settle a debt that didn't exist!" Jackson gave her a gentle shake.

"What are you going to do?" she asked, cringing as his expression grew ominous.

"Take you safely home," he replied distantly.

"Then what, Jackson?"

"Then my brother and I are going back to the celebration. It's party time for the Monroes."

11

"I ABSOLUTELY REFUSE to make one step toward home," Emaline cried. "Not one more step, I tell you!"

"Which is why, wife, I've confiscated your shoes and you are riding," Jackson stated with resolve as he marched along the sidewalk toward the Holt house. Emaline had begun to sputter about retribution about a block and a half ago, insistent on going directly to the park with him in search of Dooley. That was when Jackson neutralized her forcibly, hoisting her over his shoulder like a sack of flour, her moon facing the one in the sky that so intrigued her.

"I've managed just fine alone without you!" she blurted out breathlessly as she bounced along.

"You've proven very resourceful," he complimented. "But this is a showdown I'd rather face alone."

"Why? It's my life's he's tampered with."

"And mine!" he spat out bitterly. "My plan simply will not work with you there."

"Evenin', Emaline!" an elderly male voice piped up from a nearby porch.

Emaline lifted her head, parting the tide of blond hair in her eyes. "Evenin', Mr. Hoffman. Missed you at the picnic."

"Touch of the rheumatism in my knees. Saw the fireworks though from here."

"They were . . . very nice. About this . . ." she ventured to explain.

"Never you mind, m'dear. Him being another Monroe and all. At least you got an engagement ring this time."

"The old coot," Jackson muttered crossly.

"Never mind him, Jackson," Emaline hissed. "What are you going to do?"

"It's another one of those masculine things we spoke of the other day."

"It is my honor and my business!"

The click, click of Jackson's boots on the pavement was the only sound for a brief time. He finally answered in matter-of-fact determination. "I'm going to scare the hell out of him."

"Very well, Jackson," Emaline acquiesced in a sigh. "You're more than well suited for the task."

Jackson swung left at the Holts' front walk, tramped up the wooden porch stairs and yanked open the screen door with a squeak. The entry was dim, lit only by a stream of moonlight. There was lamplight glowing in the parlor however. One bulb bright enough to silhouette Verna's ample figure in the doorway. She was dressed for bed in her ruffled flannel nightgown.

Why, oh, why, hadn't she hit the sack yet? Jackson inwardly lamented, glancing at the clock on the wall. It was past one.

"Home, are you?" Verna said stonily to the man filling the front entrance. The only sound in the house was the screen door snapping back in place. He seemed ten feet tall at that moment, Emaline slung over his sturdy shoulder, his eyes glittering wildly, his face shaded with whiskers.

"Put her down," Verna ordered icily, moving out of the shadows.

Jackson complied, setting Emaline on the floor, handing her her shoes. She looked especially small with her feet bare and her hair mussed, dwarfed by the huge leather jacket enveloping her torso.

"Auntie . . ." Emaline began, raising a hand out of one long sleeve.

Verna approached the pair, the beady eyes marble and menacing. "I took the liberty of turning your cards, Emaline."

"Oh?" Emaline quavered.

"You shouldn't have bothered, Verna," Jackson cut in curtly.

"Oh, it was no trouble atall," she assured in sarcastic sweetness. "Would you like to hear, *poshrat*?"

Emaline took one look at the cards clenched in her aunt's plump hand and shuddered. "No, I've had enough fortune for one night."

"Oh, but you shall hear," Verna proclaimed, flipping over the first card, raising it to them.

"Jack of hearts!" Emaline gasped, pressing a hand to her mouth.

"Jack of hearts," Verna agreed, then went on to recite the interpretation in bellowing theatrical form. "Beware of Cupid's little darts. Your fate is held by the knave of hearts."

Emaline unconsciously backed up a step, to find Jackson's arm solidly at her back.

Verna flipped the second card. "Jack of clubs," she announced. "Eyes of gray, hair spun gold, two strong arms about you fold."

"Enough," Emaline pleaded with a cringe.

"Only one more," Verna promised coldly, stepping closer.

"Another Jack?" Jackson demanded, a sardonic curl to his mouth.

"Better," Verna assured coldly. She flipped up the seven of clubs under her niece's nose, bringing a cry of mortification to Emaline's lips. "His words are fair, his hair is black. Turn to the one whose name is Jack!"

"My hair is auburn like yours," Jackson protested coolly. The only outward sign of his simmering temper was the throbbing pulse at his throat.

"It's close enough, you rogue!"

"It makes no sense, Auntie," Emaline intervened in an attempt to salvage her swiftly crumbling pyramid of lies. "Hair of gold, then black."

"Not alone it doesn't. But put all his fortunes together and what do you have but the original Jackson Monroe!" Verna exploded, hurling the cards at him.

"Alive and well at your service," Jackson assented with a slight mocking bow as the cards fell at the toes of his boots. He calmly reached over to dig into the top pocket of his leather jacket centered just below his beloved rapidly beating heart, and extracted a cigar and matches. He clamped the stogie between his teeth and struck a flame to it. "Jackson Monroe, handyman-husband at your service, dear Auntie," he proclaimed after a long indolent puff.

"Blackguard! Rattlesnake!" Contempt flowed from Verna's mouth like a river of rage. "Pettifogger!" she added in a grope for the worst.

"Pettifogger?" He laughed mockingly. "I am not an unscrupulous lawyer, I am not lawyer at all!"

She paused in a movement of dumbfoundment. "Oh, that is right!" she seethed. "'Twas Lindy's work, if I recall."

"Margaret?" she yelled up the staircase. "Come quickly! We've been robbed! Bring Lindy with you!"

"Robbed?" Mother and daughter exclaimed in unison minutes later as they scampered down the steps on bare feet, obviously roused from slumber.

"Yes, we've been robbed," Verna confided in a shattered voice. "We've been robbed of our precious John, our fairy-tale knight. Emaline and Lindy are in cahoots on this shameful charade," she accused sternly.

Margaret paused on the bottom step, Lindy peeking over her shoulder with a mischievous twinkle.

"How many times, Margaret, have I told you that the cards never lie?" Verna lectured, pointing to the ones scattered on the floor.

"Several hundred times, Verna," Margaret replied unhappily, stifling a yawn. "What is the meaning of this?" Her eyes skated from her rumpled-looking daughter to the man looming beside her.

"The leaves never lie, either," Verna instructed. "It is only an old whimsical fool who cannot see what is standing before her. We are such fools, Margaret. Made fools by this impostor, by your own daughters!"

"I happen to be the real thing," Jackson roared, causing them all to fall silent. "I am no knight in shining armor. This is no fairy tale."

Margaret reluctantly turned to Jackson, inspecting him from his soiled knees to his wrinkled red shirt to his whiskers, to his fading red head surrounded in a cloud of smoke. "You . . ." She grasped the railing as realization seeped in. Without the aid of tea leaves or cards, she came to see that there was only one Monroe man, after all.

"It's the moonstruck curse!" Emaline lamented, grasping his arm.

"No it is not, Emaline!" he scoffed darkly, his patience gone. "Our problems are very easily pinned to earthly interference, to silly misunderstandings."

"What is the meaning of all this?" Margaret demanded in disbelief. "Jackson Monroe, you are not dead? Why are you playing this cruel masquerade?"

"I believe Emaline can supply you with those answers," he curtly assured her. "I have some unfinished business to attend to." He turned to Emaline, cupping her face in his hands. "I will be back."

"We are doomed," she lamented starkly. "We made love under the moon and our life is in ruins."

"Nonsense!"

"How can we ever be happy with this torment stalking us?"

"You said you trusted me, wife!"

"You said our love was stronger," she whispered intimately as if they were alone. "It seems you were wrong. We have no control over such powers of the universe."

"Let's rise from the ruins," he proposed anxiously. "We'll move on, away from all of these prejudices."

"History is repeating itself," she groaned, squeezing her temples. "You are leaving again. Fifteen minutes in your real skin and you're giving up!"

"You are the one surrendering," Jackson concluded grimly, his heart constricting in his chest.

"You act as if I have a choice in the matter," she said, blinking back the tears.

"You can enlarge your scope, wife. Get a taste of the world. Aren't you even a little curious about what life is like elsewhere?"

"I don't see how we can possibly make things work— so much is against us," she said mournfully.

"This time it is your wish, Emaline," he proclaimed flatly.

"It is my wish, as well," Verna bellowed. "I've packed your things. They are at the pantry door. Get out, get out, you cur!"

Jackson stormed through the house, slung his duffel bag over the same shoulder on which his wife had ridden, and jerked open the kitchen door. The last cries he heard echoing down the hallway were concerning Puff-Puff and her real and true identity.

Colin's backyard light switched on before Jackson was halfway across the lawn. "Been expecting you, chum," he greeted, pushing open the screen door. "Since I couldn't be the source of this latest tirade, I figured it was you, my fellow black-hearted cur."

Jackson stepped inside the service porch, setting his duffel bag against the dryer. "I didn't expect to be cashing in on that favor you owe me so soon," he began apologetically.

"I suppose you can stay for tonight," Colin relented, drawing a full yawn.

Jackson noticed for the first time that Colin was wearing a robe over some striped pajamas. "Look, uh, pal. My favor is of a tall order."

"I concede that you were a tremendous help getting the potion book," Colin said to placate Jackson.

"And John kept them from filing charges against you," Jackson informed him.

"Really?" he queried in surprise. "How kind. So what sort of service do you need?"

"It seems that Dooley has been extorting Emaline's waitressing services these past months by claiming I left a debt of seven grand behind. Claimed I was responsible for that fire of his."

"Hallo!" Colin reeled in shock.

"I need you to help me settle the score, right now while the moon is full."

"I'll do it, Jackson," Colin proclaimed. "I'll do it for that poor, sweet girl. Come inside. I'll change."

"You change while I scrub my hair here in your washtub." Jackson moved to the large sink, picking up a brown bar of soap.

"That's for ring around the collar," Colin protested, lifting a gray brow in doubt.

"I need something strong and fast." Jackson stripped off his shirt and turned to the faucet. "Also, we need your shears, or your shaver—whatever you use to cut your own hair."

His eyes glinted in disdain. "Why, I never—"

"Everybody in the whole blasted town knows you never go to the local barber!" Jackson interrupted impatiently. "If you're planning to change your image from recluse to Romeo, you'll have to spiff up a bit."

"You may have a point," the Brit surrendered. "I suppose you want the closely clipped Jackson Monroe cut."

"Whatever you can manage."

"Well, you just scrub away while I change, and we'll see what we can do."

Thirty minutes later, when Colin held a mirror to Jackson's face, he saw perfection. "Wonderful job."

"Not a bad cut, considering we're outside in the moonlight at two o'clock in the morning." Colin whisked the bath towel from Jackson's chest and shook it in the night air. "Now what?"

Jackson rose from the old stool where he'd been perched and ran a comb through his golden crop of hair. "I change my clothes and you go off in search of Dooley."

Colin looked at him sharply. "At this time of night?"

"He'll no doubt be around the park, tanked up on beer, pinching ladies' bottoms or dancing with a tree."

"And?"

"You bring him to his café. Tell him you thought you saw something inside."

"Someone, you mean," Colin corrected.

"No, tell the superstitious snake you saw something. Hustle him over there, discouraging any call to the sheriff."

"Right ho." Colin grinned.

"I STILL SAY we shoulda got the sheriff!"

Jackson heard Dooley's slurred protest echo down the deserted street a short time later. It sounded as if Dooley's tongue was twice as large as his mouth. It appeared by his stumbling step that his feet were twice as large as his shoes. This was no surprise to Jackson, considering the way the café owner had been swilling the beer earlier on. Jackson took a cautious look from his hiding spot as Colin took a jiggle on the front door knob.

"Shee, told ya it was locked up good and pepper," Dooley snorted.

"You aren't listening, old chap," Colin said, a coaxing timbre in his voice. "I'm not at all certain we're dealing with a physical force here."

"You think we're busting a ghost?"

Jackson nodded in grim satisfaction. Dooley's liquor-logged brain was feeding on his superstitious nature and pumping him with enough false courage to take action.

"I, ah, believe anything can happen," Colin said, leaving all options open.

"Why you want to help me?" Dooley barked, stabbing Colin's chest.

"Well, I'm considering basing a book on the supernatural," Colin openly improvised. "Tip Top Bear tracks spirits, or some such thing," he gestured off with a thin hand.

Dooley hooted with laughter. "Hey, hey, Collie, I'd love to be in a book!"

"Open the door, Mr. Dooley. And do not call me Collie," he added, his consternation apparent.

"Yeah, yeah." Dooley grumbled, inserting the key in the lock. "Anybody home?" he hollered, barging in with Colin at his heels.

The moonlight did a splendid job of illuminating the café with an eerie glow. Dooley shuffled down the aisle for a look around, and when he turned, Jackson was atop the counter, as if he'd grown right out of the orange Formica.

"It's . . . it's shou!" Dooley pointed a hammy finger up at him, his blunt features contorted in fear—a fear so profound that it sent quivers through the man's egg-shaped body.

"It's me, Dooley." Jackson gazed down at him with a granite expression, his gray eyes glinting silver madness. "Come back to set you straight."

Drunk or sober, believer or non, there was no denying that the man standing before them was Jackson Monroe, dressed in one of his white trademark T-shirts and snug faded jeans, black leather gloves on his large hands, his boots soundly planted between the condiments and napkin holder.

"You're dead!" When Dooley tried to reach for the salt-shaker, Jackson took pleasure in stepping on his meaty hand.

"I left some unfinished business behind," Jackson explained, a certain thrill of vengeance in his voice as he ground Dooley's hand under his sole.

"An apparition, to be sure," Colin piped up in mock amazement.

"Apparitions are supposed to be light and airy," Dooley babbled, attempting to wrench his hand free.

"How do you know?" Colin demanded. "He managed to walk through your locked door, did he not?"

Jackson grinned as Colin shot him a puzzled look. The Brit himself was wondering how he'd done it. "Handy in death as I was in life," Jackson muttered mirthlessly.

"Leave me alone, Monroe. I didn't hurt you."

"It is my Emaline that you've been harassing, slimeball."

"It is your brother John who has probably seduced her this very night," Dooley rushed on to lay blame. The more he tugged at his hand, the harder Jackson stepped down on it. "Touching your woman, Jackson."

"You wished to touch her," Jackson roared in remonstration. "You also used her for financial gain, tricking her into working here for nothing."

Sweat sprang from Dooley's huge face as he looked at his purple fingers, then up to Jackson's venomous features. "I only wished to claim her as my own," Dooley rattled on. "She is so lovely, so fresh."

"That is how you treat women?" Jackson spat out, his fists clenched at his sides. His body was coiled, ready to spring on its prey at any moment. "Force them into slavery?"

"What do you want?" Dooley finally asked in a slur of pain.

"I want your hide!" Jackson thundered, whacking the triple-bulb light fixture over Dooley's head with a leather-clad fist. Still held in place by Jackson's foot, he was showered by glass. Once the fragments had settled, Jackson continued in a low, lethal tone. "But I will settle for Emaline's back pay."

"But I don't have it!"

"Liar! I built that safe in back myself, remember?"

"Yes, you . . . you must be him," Dooley said in despair. "I will get the money. Please, please, let me go."

Jackson lifted his foot from Dooley's hand, kicking the saltshaker through the air with the square toe of his boot. "There's your protection, Dooley, there scattered across the floor. Lap it up for good luck if you wish. You're going to need it."

Dooley sidestepped the salt and rounded the counter to the safe in back. Jackson leaped off his perch, landing right behind him with a thud. Dooley whimpered in fear. "Don't hurt me, Monroe."

"And what mercy did you have on my Emaline?" Jackson thrust a finger at the false cupboard that held the safe. "Open it up. Now."

Dooley's fingers fumbled at the combination beneath Jackson's watchful eye. "I want a moment to count my assets. . . ."

"Everything in there, Dooley? Guess you can't trust the banks these days, with employees like Evie Jo clerking."

"Why, ah—"

"The bogus promissory note is no doubt there, too. I want it." Jackson was aware that Colin was lurking behind him, probably wearing the driest of smirks. Jackson prayed the Brit wouldn't give anything away. Once the safe was open, Jackson grabbed the collar of Dooley's bright yellow shirt and yanked him aside. Squatting on his knees, he riffled through Dooley's papers and cash. "Let me see. Eight months of pay. I figure ten grand to be close enough, that plus any tips she managed to take home, brings her into the ballpark of meagerly fair pay." Jackson stuffed the majority of the money into his jeans pocket, tossing the rest over his shoulder.

"What, this is chicken feed!" Dooley screeched, scooping up leftover bills.

"Here's the promissory note," Jackson announced, stuffing that into another pocket. "I suggest you advise Evie Jo on the laws concerning forging bank papers. A nastier woman than Emaline would make certain you were both brought up on charges."

"But you don't exist! How could you turn us in?" Dooley snarled as Jackson rose to his feet.

"Your sore hand should long be a reminder that I can rise from the grave with powerful force anytime I please," Jackson tersely warned, seizing the shorter man by the shoulders, causing slivers of glass to fall from his oily head. "Whether I'm here, or brother John's here, or Emaline is on her own with her family. You keep your grubby paws off her forever. Remember that I'll be watching your every move. As a matter of fact," he revised, "I think it best you literally move. Shut down this barn and get the hell out of town." Jackson released him with a shove and stormed for the door. To his relief, Colin waited a good few minutes before meeting up with him down a side street.

"You got him!" Colin joyously proclaimed with a hearty slap on the back.

Jackson's face crumpled in anguish. "I did what I could for Emaline. Even if she doesn't want me any longer, she can finally live without fear in the town she loves so much. Me, I'm outta here tomorrow."

"THIS VACUUM CLEANER come over on the *Mayflower*?"

Colin smiled at Jackson from his small kitchen dinette the following morning, where he was sipping coffee. "I wouldn't know, chum. I'm the first Sinclair in my brood to make the crossing. Now, stop fiddling with that contraption and sit down for a spot of breakfast."

Jackson looked down at the canister vac currently torn to pieces, then shot an apologetic smile to Colin. "Sorry I went so far. I just couldn't sleep and thought I'd do some cleaning."

"Well, I for one needed the rest and am damn grateful that the old thing didn't start. Don't worry about that mess. There's a fix-it shop in town with a man who does nothing but tinker."

Jackson sank into the other wooden chair with a heavy sigh. He looked rough, with his mussed hair and unkempt beard, dressed only in a pair of tattered jeans. Every other piece of his clothing was at that moment churning away in the washer out back, in preparation for travel.

"So, how about an egg?" Colin suggested, gesturing to the griddle on the stove. "I can whip up another in minutes."

"No, this coffee is fine." Jackson reached for the percolator on the table and filled a mug.

"So, are you ever going to tell me now how you got into that locked café last night?" Colin demanded, his aristocratic features alight with playfulness.

"After you, Colin."

"After I what?" the Brit prodded.

"I mean, I came in after you," Jackson explained, a genuine grin tugging at the corners of his mouth.

"Aha!"

"You and Dooley were so intent on what was supposed to be inside that it was easy to slip out of the grocer's doorway and sneak in right on your heels."

"Things are rarely what they seem," Colin marveled with a shake of his head.

"True, true," Jackson sulked. "Speaking for myself and my brother John."

"Jackson, you are going to have to make some solid decisions about your future," Colin proclaimed, pounding on the table. "You will either have to gracefully accept that Emaline is out of your life for good, or hasten back over there."

"Neither option interests me! Imagine, staking your fate on a moon curse," he said in disbelief.

"Imagine toiling away for months on end in that grease pit of Dooley's to pay off your debt."

"A debt she should've known I'd have never abandoned."

"You abandoned her—why not the note?" Colin relentlessly reasoned. "To an insulated girl like Emaline, the threat was real. There was an official bank note. Margaret raised her to respect authority. And there was your flight, so suspiciously close to the fire."

Jackson rubbed his eyes, muttering in despair. "None of it would've happened if she hadn't buried me!"

"Dooley still would've pulled the same flimflam, I imagine, had she truthfully announced your departure," Colin wagered. "As long as you were gone, I think he would've considered her fair game."

"Proud sorceress!"

"Fragile enchantress," Colin murmured.

"Scheming temptress!" Anger rocketed through him with missile force. "I am an honest man by nature, Colin.

I knew from the start this scheme would come to no good. Still I played along. It just wasn't like me at all."

"The bewilderment in your own voice should be clue enough," Colin asserted.

"Huh?" Jackson cast him a hazy, red-eyed look across the table.

"You've been bewitched and beguiled by a most comely maiden. Those women over there..." Colin jabbed a finger toward the Holt house. "All four of them are mysterious, mischievous and completely enrapturing. If I did wish to marry, I'd have to look no further than my own backyard."

"You really like me, limey?" a voice piped up over the hum of the washer.

Colin's head snapped to the service porch where Lindy stood bold as brass, covered in bangles and dressed in a violet-and-black knit dress with a short, flouncy skirt. "You forgot your britches, young lady!" he chided. "And you shouldn't eavesdrop on private conversations."

"This is a dress, limey. Right out of the catalog. So, what you were sayin'?"

"That you, young lady, are tart and smart," he continued, his voice softening as he added. "And a delightful adversary whom I would miss dearly."

"You goin' somewhere?" she demanded anxiously.

"No, though I entertained the idea for twenty-four hours after Verna's dressing-down. No, I've ultimately decided to remain in this edge-of-the-world burg. I made scads of new friends at the harvest moon celebration last night, garnered many dinner invitations. I believe I'm a local celebrity of sorts."

"You've been kind of growing on me of late," Lindy confessed sweetly, dimpling. "Now that I know you haven't been extorting anything other than meals from our family, I believe you're an interesting pal. And your newfound success should cut down on the mooching."

"Was I considered a suspect in Emaline's trials?" Colin's pale eyes snapped to Jackson.

"I kept my options open in the beginning," Jackson honestly admitted. "You were such delightful company for the ladies, I wondered if Emaline wasn't helping you out financially to keep this place afloat."

"A flattering dodge if I ever heard one," Colin conceded in a chuckle. "So, Lindy, to what do we owe this intrusion?"

"I didn't intrude," she cried in affront. "I knocked."

"Perhaps," Colin sighed with an eye roll.

"I came over here to cheer you guys up," she announced, her dark eyes shining.

"What is Emaline doing?" Jackson asked abruptly.

"She just woke up. Got madder than a wet hen when I told her Mother went off to see Dooley."

"She go alone?" Jackson asked her piercingly.

"Sure, Mother knows him from way back when. Said Emaline dared not ever go near him again."

"You mustn't worry about Margaret," Colin insisted. "She is merely visiting the ruins of a broken man now. Thanks to you."

"What does he mean, Jackie?" Lindy demanded excitedly, waving her bangled arms.

"I took care of everything last night," Jackson informed her gruffly, rising from his chair to roam the kitchen like a caged lion.

Lindy scampered up to him, resting her head on his bare chest. "I love you so much, boomerang boy. I knew you could fix things if you knew what to fix."

Jackson patted her kinky black head. "I want you to do something for me, little sister."

"Anything you say."

Jackson moved over to the cupboard and extracted the wad of bills and promissory note, wrapped in a rubber band. "Give this to Emaline. It's her back pay from the Tip Top and the forged note. Your family can decide what they're going to do about Dooley and Evie Jo."

"And if we need a good attorney?" Lindy asked.

"I suggest you consult the yellow pages," Jackson grunted, kicking aside the vacuum and stomping out of the room. He could hear Lindy anxiously quizzing the Brit in his wake, but it didn't matter, nothing mattered much anymore.

"WONDERFUL NEWS, Emaline!" Verna was enthusing next door, bursting out onto the front porch with a volume of the encyclopedia under her fleshy arm.

Emaline seated on the wooden steps with chin in hand, merely shrugged with disinterest.

"Gerbils are quite nice, after all. Graceful creatures who never bite unless they're mistreated. Not cuddly, mind you, but a favored pet to many a child."

"What?" Emaline mumbled despondently.

"Colin, it seems, was quite clever in choosing the gerbil to showcase my life," Verna bubbled in a glorious mood. "Children will most certainly respect the Romany ways through the eyes of the lovable Gypsy Gerbil." Verna plopped her padded seat down beside Emaline on the step. "Are you hearing me, *posh*? I've been rethinking my position with Colin," she reiterated. "I believe I'm quite keen on the idea of being immortalized in book form."

"Must seem like a more attractive offer with half the town's women vying for your place on the printed page," Emaline said bluntly.

"It's not like you to be so sour," Verna chastised, her dark eyes narrowing beneath strategically set auburn pin curls. "But your behavior of late has been atrocious, due, of course, to Jackson Monroe's influence! You girls were very naughty in your subterfuge." Verna paused in obvious anticipation of an apology, which was not forthcoming. "Margaret thinks I should join professional forces with Colin if he'll have me. Be his co-conspirator—or some such."

"I believe she said consultant," Emaline corrected on a heavy sigh.

"Yes, that was it!" She shook her head, deeply immersed in her own trials and tribulations. "Now that Colin has declared his wish to remain a bachelor, we've agreed that the rivalry is over. But I don't know...maybe down the way, I can smuggle in a little romance. I've found a new incantation in one of the old books—"

"My life has fallen apart," Emaline finally cried out, "and you're talking about spells and gerbils!"

"Jackson Monroe is a scalawag," Verna erupted crossly. "He played a monstrous trick on us."

"I told you last night that John was my invention."

Verna inhaled one of her homily-size breaths, only to be interrupted by the sharp tap of a car horn. Margaret waved as she eased the family's dark sedan into the driveway. She halted the car near the corner of the house and emerged from the driver's side, dressed for town in a powder blue shirtwaist. Lindy must have heard her, as well, for she came loping across the lawn from Colin's house.

"What happened, Mother?" Emaline asked as the pair joined them.

"Let me catch my breath on the swing," Margaret declared.

"Did he upset you?" Emaline asked, popping up so her mother could pass. "I knew I should have come along!"

Margaret settled back on the creaky swing, making room for Verna. She tilted her head back, closing her eyes for a moment. "Don't worry about me, Emaline. I was upset before I left home, remember?"

"So, Margaret, what did the evil-eyed buzzard have to say?" Verna prompted.

Margaret's eyes held a twinkle when she reopened them. "He said nothing. He's gone."

12

"THE BUZZARD melted into the street," Verna deduced with a satisfied snort.

"No. According to Little Lillian, he left the old-fashioned way," Margaret reported. "In his old pickup truck with every possession he could carry. Apparently some folks saw him struggling with his belongings and pitched right in to help. There is already a For Sale sign in the Tip Top window, for the entire building, including his upstairs apartment."

"Hurrah!" Lindy cheered.

"To tell you the truth, I felt a trifle let down."

"Why ever, Mother?" Emaline asked in amazement. She felt light as air over the news.

"Because I wanted to punch him in the nose!" Margaret sputtered in disgust.

Emaline laughed with relief. "It's over. That's the main thing."

"This certainly is an extraordinary turn of circumstances," Verna marveled. "Last night we heard the worst of him from Emaline, and now, before we had to deal with him, he's gone."

"It's not so extraordinary when you know the facts," Lindy chirped, hoisting herself up on the brown railing. She smiled with delight when all eyes riveted to her. "Jackson took care of Dooley," she reported proudly. "Went over there last night and scared the begeebees out of him. According to Colin, Jackson pretended he was an apparition from the great beyond, back to settle the score." She fluttered her hands over her head, her jewelry clinking. "The fat old creep deflated like a balloon."

"That precious man," Emaline said softly, her eyes brimming with tenderness and passion. "I drove him away and he still salvaged my honor."

"Verna and I drove him away," Margaret corrected with quiet firmness, immediately backed with a humph from Verna. "And I don't see how we can regret it. He is the second rambler to clomp through our lives like a tractor through a rosebed."

"Don't compare him with Father!" Emaline took them to task, girding herself with resolve. Her mother received her words like a blow, leaning back in the swing. "Jackson did the honorable thing. He came back for me! In less than a year's time he was back full of apology. And what did I do? I turned him into a man I thought you'd admire! He didn't want to deceive you, I made him do it."

"But you thought you were protecting him from the law, Emaline!" Lindy broke in.

"I truly did," Emaline said, patting her sister's shoulder. "But I was guilty of trying to mold John into the man of your dreams, ladies. And what a success he was!"

"He enjoyed it," Verna said in lofty reproof.

"Why shouldn't he?" Emaline shot back reproachfully. "He basked in your approval, your praise. We're the closest thing he'd ever had to hearth and home."

"He still should've owned up to everything," Margaret insisted.

"He wanted to," Emaline wailed. "I wouldn't let him. I couldn't risk the law coming after him with that note."

"And what have you, Emaline, after working for that monster Dooley for all those months?" Verna challenged.

"I've—we've had the monthly income Jackson's sent," Emaline faltered. "The money I claimed was from Dooley."

"She's got her back wages, too," Lindy announced, extracting the wad of bills out of her dress pocket. "Ten grand in five-hundred-dollar bills." Lindy basked in the oohs and ahs as Emaline weighed the roll in her hand. "The promissory note is there, too."

"Jackson made amends the best he could." Emaline choked back the rush of tears, intent on making her point. "Can't you see that the qualities you loved in John are part of Jackson? Remember when we were seated out here the other night, Mother, and you were talking about having a second chance with John, that maybe you were too hard on Jackson? I want my second chance to make this right with him. Both of you understand about love. Even though you made light of your duel over Colin, you know as well as I that you both would jump at the chance to marry him."

"We've only wanted the best for you girls," Margaret replied, tears rimming her eyes. "Verna and I don't agree on much, but a Prince Charming for you two is our mutual dream."

"Jackson may not be your idea of a prince, but he is mine," she softly reprimanded, dropping to her knee at the swing. "He's accepted my Romany ways the best he could, accepted my superstitious nature... Oh, what am I saying?" she cried out in anguish. "No matter how you feel, there is still the curse of the moon hanging over this family. I cannot again draw Jackson into our jinxed existence. If something happened to him because of it, I'd never forgive myself."

"Well, surely Auntie can find some remedy for that stinkin' old thing," Lindy assured with a firm nod.

"I've asked her, Lindy," Emaline told her with a grateful smile. "She just says it's something our parents had to live with."

"Perhaps I have been unfair to Jackson," Margaret admitted with reluctance. "I've been prejudiced because of Willie. Regardless, it is your life, Emaline." Margaret reached down to stroke her daughter's head. "I feel so terrible about all of this that even as a nonbeliever, Emaline, I will help you search through Willie's old books for an antidote. Whatever it takes to ease your mind. Verna shall lead us in our quest."

"I only put you off this because I didn't want you expecting to somehow summon back your father, *posh*," Verna quavered in her off-key soprano. "After all these years, it seemed wise to leave things alone."

"I didn't tell you my true reasons for asking, Auntie, because I was shielding Jackson's identity," Emaline pointed out patiently.

"Hey, we gotta hurry up," Lindy urged, hopping off the railing. "Colin thinks Jackson's too spent to leave this afternoon, but he might be going tonight, while the moon is still bright."

Verna wrung the bejeweled hands in her lap as all eyes fell upon her. "We needn't hurry," she confessed, glancing sheepishly at Emaline.

Emaline rose to her feet, hovering over the cherished aunt who had taught her so much. "Why? It's not like you to give up on anything!"

"Believe me, in the early days I never dreamed this curse would mushroom into anything so crucial in your life, Emaline."

"But it has, Aunt Verna!" Emaline prodded. "I've centered all of my marital misfortune on this one curse. I simply must have the antidote."

Verna, suddenly zapped of her vigor, waved a limp hand. "You . . . you won't need it, *posh*," she mumbled. "There is no moonstruck curse."

Cries of astonishment filled the morning air.

"Of course there is," Emaline denied.

"I for one suspected there was not," Margaret asserted, casting a reproving look at the woman seated beside her. "All those years you were covering for Willie's desertion with that wild tale of the moon. I believe a man should face up to the consequences of his actions—as Jackson has."

"I did it for Willie, yes," Verna confessed. "I did it for myself as well. I thought the girls might not love me, love our heritage if they didn't look kindly on their father's memory."

"We all love you," Margaret grudgingly assured her.

"How dare you call Jackson names, take me to task for lying, when you've told the whopper of them all?" Emaline flared resentfully. "I could've made love to my husband the second he walked in the door, had I known! We could've gotten on with our lives without the pressure of that stupid curse!"

Verna dissolved into tears, extracting her hanky from the bosom where Jackson Monroe used to live. "I am so sorry, Emaline."

"We'll do anything to help," Margaret consoled, rising from the swing to embrace her eldest.

"How do you win back a husband who's offered you his love twice?" Emaline challenged in a sob against her mother's shoulder. "How do you bewitch an angry, bitter man whose heart and pride were stomped upon by four conniving females?"

"Ah!" Verna proclaimed, her dark eyes bright beneath the tears. "Now for that, my dear Emaline, there are truly many antidotes!"

SWEET, SWEET SLEEP.

Jackson had dozed off sometime in midafternoon in Colin's backyard hammock. Strung between two large oak trees, it comfortably cocooned the long, powerful man as surely as a cradle would a newborn. Sunlight dappled through the thin veil of remaining leaves, warming his face and arms, the last hurrah to his farmer's tan. An occasional breeze wafted through the yard, a soothing counterpoint to the blaze above.

There had been nothing mellow about his mood when Jackson, at Colin's urging, had crawled into the green fabric folds of the outdoor bed. Moments after he'd stretched out, he began to feel his pulse slacken, his eyelids droop. He was running on empty physically and emotionally. He was plain worn-out.

Jackson slept on, his mind blissfully devoid of skittering visions of Gypsy razzle-dazzle and tortured dreams of lost love. He was floating for an indeterminate amount of time. Until . . .

The restless invasion.

Hushed distant whispers teased him. Fingers of wind ruffled his hair. Or fingers of another sort . . . Damnation, it was happening again!

Jackson snapped open his eyes to find the moon gleaming down on him. The moon and a pair of dark mischievous eyes. He'd slept into the night. "What time is it?" he demanded sleepily.

"Ten-thirty," Lindy answered with a forlorn pout. "Why are you always so disappointed to see me?"

"Truly a mystery, little sister," he fired back gruffly. "This is where you came in the first time around, remember? On the count of three, I want you to skedaddle. One, two—"

"Oh, quit your fussin'." With an indulgent huff, Lindy leaned over the hammock, raised a tiny scissors to his head, and cleanly snipped a tuft of hair from his head. "This is all I wanted, Jackie."

But was it the first lock or the last? With heart-thudding trepidation Jackson sat up in the tippy hammock, his hands flying to his hair for inventory. All there. It was still all there!

"Don't be such a suspicious poop," Lindy complained, placing a stilling hand on his shoulder as he threatened to tip over. "I only needed the one lock for my putsi."

"I shudder to ask, but . . ."

Lindy pressed her fingers to her mouth with a giggle. "I am speaking of this red silk pouch. It just wouldn't be magical without your lock." She stuffed the hair inside the bag and drew the string closure tight.

Jackson arched a brow. "What else is in there? What does it mean?"

Lindy tipped her head toward the illuminated sky, taking mental inventory. "Your pouch here contains a lodestone, touch of myrrh, small feather from a robin, and of course, rosemary leaves."

"It is your pouch," Jackson snapped with a stony expression, folding his arms across his flannel-covered chest.

"The second the hair hit rosemary, it became yours," Lindy told him with a coy smirk.

"So what is it?" Jackson asked again. "Some kind of bon voyage gift?"

"The very opposite!" Lindy proclaimed in genuine dismay. "Do you think we wish to dispose of you?"

"Bury a man once, and he's of a leery nature."

"It is a lure from Emaline," Lindy hastily placated. "She stitched the pouch, so it is her spell. Once your hair was added, your fate was set on a course of her choosing."

"What course is that?" he asked flatly, though his heart was ramming in his rib cage. The idea that she was up to something again stirred his emotions, sending euphoric surges through his system. He was wide-awake now!

"Don't you feel the urge to do something?" she asked anxiously.

"Indeed I do, little sister," he confided, with a wicked curl to his mouth. "You been paddled lately?"

Lindy stepped back out of his reach with a laugh. "I mean, don't you feel a draw to your wife?"

He needed no spell for that! "I always feel such a draw," he stated simply, arms folded across his chest.

"Surely it must seem stronger than ever now!" she prodded.

"As a matter of fact," he pondered in his characteristic honesty, "it does."

"Then I shall simply hook this pouch on a string around your neck—"

"Give me the blasted thing!" Jackson slid off the hammock, snatched the red silk bag, crumbled it in his fist and marched across the lawn.

"That pouch should help you home in on her straightaway!" Lindy called after him.

Jackson waved a careless hand in his wake. Tracking Emaline's scent had never ever been a problem before.

"HONEY, YOU'RE HOME."

Jackson halted in his tracks at the third-level bathroom door, unprepared for the scene awaiting him. The room was dim, lit only by three stout flickering candles on the vanity. A bowl full of crushed leaves sat on the windowsill. Light, sweet-smelling incense wafted in the air. Emaline herself looked truly a goddess, stretched out in the claw-footed tub, her alabaster skin slick and enticing. Her thick corn silk hair fanned her shoulders, the wispy ends grazing her rosy nipples. The sight made Jackson harden with desire, his jeans threatening to burst wide open along with his temper. How could she do this to him after driving him away? "Am I really home, Emaline?"

"Yes, Jackson, you are." Her deep, sensual voice sent a ripple of awareness through his system. She was gazing up at him longingly, her lips parted slightly, her exotic tilted eyes smoldering lustily. Though innocent to many of the harsh realities of the world, Mrs. Jackson Monroe was well schooled in the art of lovemaking, thanks to the mister. And she was using all of his own lessons to seduce him on the spot. Dashed with her magical efforts, she was obviously bound and determined in her mission of consummation.

"Where are the others—burying some bulbs upside down in the garden?" he asked stiffly. He'd searched the house top to bottom as a precaution and found it to be empty. He understood none of this, but by gawd he was going to before he fell into that bubbling tub of heaven! "Well, Emaline?"

"They have vowed to keep their noses out of our business from now on," Emaline replied with a lilt of pleasure. "They have gone forth to follow their own pleasures."

"Really?" Jackson asked in blunt amazement.

"They're in Eagle Point at this very minute inking some hot bingo cards. They've come to a new understanding with Colin and they've renewed their triangular friendship."

"Renewal is good for the soul," Jackson agreed with grim satisfaction. He rubbed a hand over his bristly face, his fingers never quite obstructing his view of Emaline. She grasped the soapy pink sponge with her left hand to scrub her collarbone, the garnet chips on her engagement ring glimmering red in the froth. Heat poured over him in waves as rivulets of water rolled and angled down between her breasts.

"I wanted to thank you for handling Dooley," Emaline ventured when he stood by silently.

"I had to make sure he wouldn't bother you again," Jackson explained quietly. "Considering how shaky our relationship is, I had to have some sort of lasting guarantee that he wouldn't harass you again, no matter what."

"Yes, you must've scared him good and proper. He's left town, with no plans of ever returning."

Hands on hips, Jackson chuckled deeply in satisfaction.

"Yes, you kept your promise," Emaline repeated with a sigh.

"I keep all my promises," Jackson claimed, his voice laced with dangerous patience. "There are some gaps in space and time...." He relented in self-recrimination, sucking in air as she raised her knees out of the water. He wanted so badly to step forward and part those creamy legs, finger her soft triangle of curls, explore deeper and deeper, urging her to cry out for complete fulfillment.

"I believe in you, Jackson," Emaline intoned, her delicate features solemn with sincerity.

"Then what is all this bag business about?" he demanded, tossing the silk pouch onto the vanity. It slid into a candle, bouncing into the sink.

"Putsi insurance," she said unevenly, her thin golden brows twitching under his glower. "I had to get you over here somehow."

The quaver beneath her bravado kept him from roaring like a lion. "How about opening the back door and calling out, 'Yoo-hoo, Jackson. Can I see you, please'?"

"I didn't think you'd want to come after the scene last night! I figured I'd need some extra oomph behind me."

"I came because you wished it, not because of some bag full of stuff."

"It is the way I do things," she contended, her black eyes blazing. "I accept you as you are. Please don't fault my magic beliefs."

"All this hocus-pocus," he growled with a sweeping gesture. "Some of it in my favor, it seems, but then there's the moon, shining over us with its curse, overshadowing everything else." He regarded her with a mocking twist to his mouth. "Have you found a cure for the curse? Is that why I'm in favor again?"

"You've never been out of favor, sweet baby," she assured, the flash of anger in her eyes glazing back to its lusty origins.

Oh, how she wanted him, Jackson realized. But he simply had to understand it all first, before he was too enveloped in her consuming aura to reason.

"Love me, Jackson," she pleaded. Resting her head back against the lip of the tub, she squeezed the sponge over her face, the water coursing down her etched cheekbones, the column of her slender throat. "After last night, I can never again be without your touch."

The ache in Jackson's heart matched his ache in his loins, causing him to nearly yowl in pain. "Why now, Emaline?" he demanded.

"Because there is nothing to stop us, sweet baby," she goaded hungrily. "I am starving for you and there are no more barriers between us."

"There is your little family curse."

"No!"

"No?" he queried, his eyes fixed on her in speculation.

"Oh, it was all a lie!" she confessed, throwing the sopping sponge full tilt at his chest, leaving a wet splotch on his plaid shirt. "Aunt Verna made it up to shield our father from shame."

"It was nothing?" Jackson erupted in mirthless laughter, staring at the sponge at his toes.

"I was going to tell you after the bath," she assured. "I just didn't want you to walk out on me tonight in a rage."

"So the old biddy made it up." Jackson gritted his teeth, casting his eyes to the ceiling.

"She didn't know it influenced us," Emaline added, watching his fingers curl and flex at his sides.

"What shall I do with you, wife?" he demanded, possessive desperation in his tone and expression.

"Lock the door, Jackson," Emaline directed simply. She twisted in the tub, reaching for the bowl on the sill behind her. "Once I add this witch hazel to the water," she warned, "you will find me irresistible. Then, my husband, you shall know what to do with me!"

"Is that what all this is about?" he asked, scanning the setup once again. His unpretentious wife thought she needed a potion pick-me-up to seduce him! His heart constricted over the guilelessness. How easily she could bring forth his rage, then his compassion. She was indeed the witch of his dreams, with no need of extra oomph!

"I must have you, Jackson," she persisted in a velvet murmur. "I will have you with any means at my disposal."

"You are already irresistible, wife, most likely to any man with a pulse. You don't need anything like this," he objected in exasperation as she poured the crushed leaves into the water.

"Lock the door, I say," she insisted in a throaty command.

Jackson shook his head in belligerence. "Aside from the magic that may or may not exist in this old world, I still contend that our passion is the strongest force in our lives."

"Never know it by your hesitation," she rasped in husky reproof.

"Just tell me you think it is so," he requested calmly, though internally he teetered on the edge of complete ungluing. Her natural musty scent was overpowering the incense now, scorching his nostrils with its sweetness. "I need to know there will never again be a curse that will hamper our bond."

"You are right. Together we are a force as volatile as any in the universe." She surrendered in a sigh that puffed her breasts a fraction. "So what do you say, sweet baby?" she challenged with a burning onyx gaze. "Are you going to lock up all the passions in here for us, or are you going to let them seep out into the rest of the house?"

Jackson leaned into the door, huffing like a steaming locomotive. "Are you going to agree to a belated cross-country honeymoon, wife?" he demanded with his last ounce of reserve.

"Seems only fair to do a bit of exploring outside of Hollow Tree. And, it so happens that I saw the journey in my teacup this very afternoon," she disclosed, lifting a drippy leg into the air, pressing her toe into the tiled wall. "I'm already packed."

"Don't move a muscle, wife," Jackson ordered, his eye never leaving her raised leg as he clicked the lock. He stripped off his clothing with lightning speed, pausing to grab the pink sponge from the floor.

"What do you say you rub my back and tell me all about the cycle trip ahead?" she tempted with a twinkle.

Jackson grasped her poised leg, sliding the sponge from her calf down the satin trail of her inside thigh. She gasped and shivered as he fell to his knee, driving the sponge beneath the wavy surface.

"Let's forget about the cycle trip just for tonight and take another sort of ride," he suggested, nuzzling her with the sponge.

"Always on the move, ramblin' man," she teased, stroking his chin with a drippy finger. She shifted in the tub, opening her knees in invitation.

He slid over the rim on top of her, pressing her deeply into the water.

"We move as one from here on in, Emaline," he groaned in promise.

"Of course," she purred thickly, arching into him. "I have the word of an honest man."

A Note From Leandra Logan

The storybook hero is a strong, sexy man with molten lips, swivel hips and seductive eyes. He's tough enough to rescue the damsel in distress, but sensitive enough to fulfill the fair one's needs and desires. In short, the white knight in shining armor.

But what of the honorable knight who has fallen? The vulnerable flesh-and-blood male who has let down his lady love?

With human error in mind, I created my fallible fellow, Jackson Monroe. On the surface, his deed seemed dastardly. He loved her and he left her. End of story. But that was the beginning of chapter one.

I was forced to explore the man with a sympathetic and empathetic eye. My sexy, rambling rogue was repentant. An honest man by nature, he was back to take his punishment. In sterling heroic tradition, he was owning up to his mistake and courting forgiveness. Not that it was going to be easy....

I sincerely doubt there are many heroes who cherish their damsels more than Jackson Monroe does his. He's hopped the fence to view both patches of grass and knows where he belongs. The act of confession lightens the soul. Subsequent forgiveness sends it soaring. Jackson Monroe would tell you so with forthright honesty.

Rebels & Rogues

Quinn: He was a real-life hero to everyone except himself.

THE MIGHTY QUINN
by Candace Schuler
Temptation #397, June 1992

All men are not created equal. Some are rough around the edges. Tough-minded but tenderhearted. Incredibly sexy. The tempting fulfillment of every woman's fantasy.

When it's time to fight for what they believe in, to win that special woman, our Rebels and Rogues are heroes at heart. Twelve Rebels and Rogues, one each month in 1992, only from Harlequin Temptation!

OVER THE YEARS, TELEVISION HAS BROUGHT
THE LIVES AND LOVES OF MANY CHARACTERS INTO
YOUR HOMES. NOW HARLEQUIN INTRODUCES YOU
TO THE TOWN AND PEOPLE OF

One small town—twelve terrific love stories.

GREAT READING...GREAT SAVINGS...AND A FABULOUS FREE GIFT!

Each book set in Tyler is a self-contained love story; together, the twelve novels stitch the fabric of the community.

By collecting proofs-of-purchase found in each Tyler book, you can receive a fabulous gift, ABSOLUTELY FREE! And use our special Tyler coupons to save on your next TYLER book purchase.

Join us for the fourth TYLER book,
MONKEY WRENCH by Nancy Martin.

Can elderly Rose Atkins successfully bring a new love into granddaughter Susannah's life?

FREE GIFT OFFER

To receive your free gift, send us the specified number of proofs-of-purchase from any specially marked Free Gift Offer Harlequin or Silhouette book with the Free Gift Certificate properly completed, plus a check or money order (do not send cash) to cover postage and handling payable to Harlequin/Silhouette Free Gift Promotion Offer. We will send you the specified gift.

FREE GIFT CERTIFICATE

ITEM	A. GOLD TONE EARRINGS	B. GOLD TONE BRACELET	C. GOLD TONE NECKLACE
# of proofs-of-purchase required	3	6	9
Postage and Handling	$1.75	$2.25	$2.75
Check one	☐	☐	☐

Name: _____

Address: _____

City: _____ State: _____ Zip Code: _____

Mail this certificate, specified number of proofs-of-purchase and a check or money order for postage and handling to: HARLEQUIN/SILHOUETTE FREE GIFT OFFER 1992, P.O. Box 9057, Buffalo, NY 14269-9057. Requests must be received by July 31, 1992.

PLUS—Every time you submit a completed certificate with the correct number of proofs-of-purchase, you are automatically entered in our MILLION DOLLAR SWEEPSTAKES! No purchase or obligation necessary to enter. See below for alternate means of entry and how to obtain complete sweepstakes rules.

MILLION DOLLAR SWEEPSTAKES
NO PURCHASE OR OBLIGATION NECESSARY TO ENTER.

To enter, hand-print (mechanical reproductions are not acceptable) your name and address on a 3″×5″ card and mail to Million Dollar Sweepstakes 6097, c/o either P.O. Box 9056, Buffalo, NY 14269-9056 or P.O. Box 621, Fort Erie, Ontario L2A 5X3. Limit: one entry per envelope. Entries must be sent via 1st-class mail. For eligibility, entries must be received no later than March 31, 1994. No liability is assumed for printing errors, lost, late or misdirected entries.

Sweepstakes is open to persons 18 years of age or older. All applicable laws and regulations apply. Sweepstakes offer void wherever prohibited by law. Prizewinners will be determined no later than May 1994. Chances of winning are determined by the number of entries distributed and received. For a copy of the Official Rules governing this sweepstakes offer, send a self-addressed, stamped envelope (WA residents need not affix return postage) to: Million Dollar Sweepstakes Rules, P.O. Box 4733, Blair, NE 68009.

✂ HT2U

ONE PROOF-OF-PURCHASE

To collect your fabulous FREE GIFT you must include the necessary FREE GIFT proofs-of-purchase with a properly completed offer certificate.

(See inside back cover for offer details)